The Last Bullet

The Last Bullet

NELSON NYE

Thorndike Press • Chivers Press
Waterville, Maine USA　Bath, England

This Large Print edition is published by Thorndike Press, USA and by Chivers Press, England.

Published in 2001 in the U.S. by arrangement with Golden West Literary Agency.

Published in 2001 in the U.K. by arrangement with Golden West Literary Agency.

U.S. Hardcover 0-7862-3394-X (Western Series Edition)
U.K. Hardcover 0-7540-4603-6 (Chivers Large Print)
U.K. Softcover 0-7540-4604-4 (Camden Large Print)

The text of this Large Print edition is unabridged.
Other aspects of the book may vary from the original edition.

Set in 16 pt. Plantin

Printed in the United States on permanent paper.

British Library Cataloguing in Publication Data available.

Library of Congress Cataloging-in-Publication Data

Nye, Nelson C. (Nelson Coral), 1907–
    The last bullet / Nelson Nye.
        p. cm.
    ISBN 0-7862-3394-X (lg. print : hc : alk. paper)
    1. Large type books.   I. Title.
PS3527.Y33 L3 2001
813′.54—dc21   2001027607

The Last Bullet

1

It was past noon.

Bright glare of sun, almost overhead, struck into the dusty streets and caromed off the walls of Naco with a glitter that made the eyeballs burn. A casual glance might have found little to choose between nearer surroundings and the backed dun surfaces that shimmered and swam beyond protection of the flag hanging limp as a gutted flounder above the rust brown of the U.S. Customs.

Dale Maffitt had run out of casual glances.

He didn't like where he was but the Mexican view held no allurements at all. He was glad to be even this little removed from it.

There was no wind, only the scorched smell of heat and the pitiless glare that fried the eyes and exposed every crevice and hoof pock and wheel rut. A thirst was in Maffitt's throat, a terrible craving for tobacco he dared not smoke. The ache of this ran all through his long body, and the itch of sweat and the cramps from standing so great a while without moving.

Those patches of shadow, like so many things lately, were liars and cheats with the blue look of coolness which could melt a man down like hog fat in a skillet. Maffitt's miseries brought vividly into his head the smooth, cultured features of Cecil Breeding, his dead father's former partner, and the sly ease with which the man had been rid of him. The whole deal smelled as Maffitt looked back on it. Behind Breeding's glib talk of the early grave Maffitt senior had drunk himself into, and the parade of debts which had wiped out Maffitt's inheritance, was something which Maffitt aimed eventually to get hold of.

Plain greed — or had there been fear lurking back of it? He had wanted to do something, Breeding implied, which might take some of the sting out of Maffitt's collapsed prospects. There was of course no stake for him at Bridle Bit but there was this horse which Breeding wanted. Belonged to some Mexican south of the Border, some government official — Olivares, Breeding said. Maffitt's father's former partner would pay three thousand American dollars for the horse. If Maffitt could acquire the stallion more cheaply he would have himself a stake.

Very neat bait.

Prior to Breeding's offer Maffitt had been three years away from the ranch, knocking about in odd corners of the land, piling up an unsavory reputation, out of one scrape and into another. This hadn't been mentioned during their talk but, with the clarity of hindsight, Maffitt realized now it had been in Breeding's mind.

He could see a lot of things now he should have thought about sooner. He had checked into his father's death; drink had done for him, no doubt about that. He was known to have borrowed from every business in town, putting up pieces of the ranch for security.

You couldn't hold that against Breeding. There was nothing illegal in buying these up — nothing off-color anywhere that Maffitt had looked, except his father had been on the wagon for years and been as down on drink as only a reformed drinker could be.

Dale had taken Breeding's offer, agreeing to see what he could do about the horse. Against better judgment he'd reluctantly allowed Breeding to advance him a third of the stipulated price — more damned money than Maffitt had ever got his hooks on. "You'll have expenses," the rancher said, brushing aside Maffitt's protests.

He'd been wrong about that; Maffitt lived off the land. And after a deal of haggling he had gotten the horse for that thousand dollars and, armed with a bill of sale, had started back to deliver the horse and collect the other two thousand dollars.

Five days ago. He'd learned a few things about Olivares since then. Two days after setting out he'd discovered dust on his backtrail. A dark hunch had taken him away from the road and sent him burrowing into adjacent hills and that dust had come right along after him.

He'd crossed a river and got into the mountains, riding by night and hiding by day. It had kept him alive despite some tight moments but it had not improved the state of his temper. Olivares had gotten the thousand agreed on but those days in the hills had made it pretty evident he had no intention of saying goodbye to the horse. They had shot Maffitt's own mount yesterday.

Afligido — that was what they called this Mexican stud — was no youngster but he had two stones and much heart. He also had bottom and an amazing early speed. He could hit full stride inside of three jumps and carry it into a half mile if he had to — he had a lot of Steeldust in him and the temper that went with it, yet you could hitch him to a hairpin once he gave you his allegiance. Maffitt had discovered before he'd gone ten miles he had got the horse for a good deal less than half its worth; it was why he'd got off that road so damned fast, and it was one of the reasons he was still on his feet.

Between scrinched lids his hard glance swept again the weathered backs of these buildings, liking them no better, moving on with a singular bitterness to study once more the plastered and unplastered portions of walls waveringly visible through the distortion of heat where the Mexican end of the twin towns' main drag faded out against the bright slope of the mountain.

Very soon now both towns — certainly Naco, Arizona — would begin to yawn and stretch and scratch their way back to tasks laid aside during these hours of midday siesta. Much as he hated making any move which might fetch Olivares' hired assassins out of their burrows he knew he could not remain here longer.

Cottonwood leaves stirred above him and trembled in a tiny breath of air, forerunner of the mid-afternoon wind that like the strike of a prodded snake would come winging up out of the land of tomorrow, flapping loose boards and loose pieces of tin while it buried this place in a fog of brown dust.

Maffitt, unfortunately, couldn't wait. He had to get himself lost in advance of that time. He'd been tempted long since to try some of those doors which loomed so invitingly, resisting the urge, knowing he was watched — perhaps not actually, but they would know where he was the moment he moved. Only for that one brief interval had he eluded them completely since illegally crossing the border in the last tattered dregs of the dark before dawn; long enough to hide Afligido but not enough by considerable to move him out of their reach.

This was all open country. They had him boxed and they knew it, content to wait even as he was for the town to shake off at least a portion of its quiet before slipping into the final stages of this matter.

Across the line, east of the garrison flag and bell tower, a man shouldered up out of a clutter of discarded packing crates, leisurely brushing himself off, glancing with a flash of teeth in the direction of Maffitt's cottonwood. One hand dipped and rose with the buff shape of a sombrero which he clapped on his head with a mocking flourish.

Casas.

Even from here Maffitt could see the

scarlet chin string of Olivares' Indian cavalry. Maffitt watched the man turn and strike off toward the street — no illegal crossing for Casas. He'd come openly through Customs, empty handed and smiling as befitted a man who was sure of his ground, filled with frijoles and confidence, the right hand of His Excellency, General Domatilio Olivares, provisional governor of Sonora.

A trumpet call came silvery mellow through the trembling leaves and Maffitt thought *Even their goddam bugles sound different!* Lazy as a love song, as though to the man on the mouthpiece time was not of the slightest significance.

Probably true.

Time was a curse of the gringo, and it was already past time for Dale Maffitt to be gone. He had not availed himself of this profusion of back doors mainly because he hadn't wished to call undue attention to these buildings. They were important to him, being close to the horse he had hidden right under their noses.

He suspected Casas could get all the help he wanted for this, no need to fetch anyone over the line. For a handful of dollars he could hire all the bravos . . .

He stared hard directly west of him.

There'd been a face back of that barrel not twenty minutes ago, another farther down. There were probably others hidden in the mesquite brush behind him; it wouldn't conceal a horse but there was plenty of cover for men on their bellies. Casas' move would be the signal. They'd be inching up now.

No change touched Maffitt's solid cheeks. Not even when a hat showed near the end of these two-floor adobes; and the ranch — Bridle Bit — was three hundred miles away.

No air now, only the glare and the heat that was like water creeping over you. Somewhere a door slammed like the crack of a pistol. A tough smile moved across Maffitt's lips. They wouldn't be using guns — not on this side. A knife or a rock could be just as effective.

He'd considered this carefully. All he needed right now was a fistful of seconds where no one could see him. Any of these shadowy slots between buildings would serve if he moved quick enough. He had to get onto the street and with enough time to spare to get clean across it before they got close to him. It wasn't his life Maffitt worried about losing but the horse.

He rubbed his half-asleep legs, working

the knots from his muscles. This had to be done while Casas was busy with Customs — he didn't want Casas' eyes pointing him out to them. The old streaky feeling ran its pulse of excitement through Maffitt. He didn't look around; with a deep in-pulled breath he ran for the alley directly in front of him.

A shout went up. Something sailed past his shoulder. Brush broke back of him. Then he was into the passage, sprinting with every last ounce of drive in him.

They had farther to go and they didn't have Maffitt's incentive. The alley was burdened with a miscellany of trash but he got through, slamming round the near corner and pulling up, breath whistling, for a scanty glance in both directions. There were a lot of wood-and-tin awnings jutting out above the walk but the street momentarily was empty. No sign of Casas or the men at Customs. Evidently that shout had hauled them back off the street.

Relief roared through Maffitt.

He was ducking forward for his dash across when a man bulged onto the planks three doors below. Maffitt hadn't any choice. The fellow had his fist back, a jagged rock ready to whiz from it and his mouth springing into the start of a yell when Maffitt threw down on him, firing from the hip. The man spun around in a crumpling fall.

The report crashed off the fronts of the buildings, swelling the clamor surging out of the alley — *no time to cross now!* Maffitt's look caught a balcony four feet above him and he jumped, fingers catching the projecting floorboards. Swinging desperately he heaved himself up, hearing sudden clatter on the planks below. Frantically scrambling he got over the low railing, crouching stiffly beneath a window as a racket of boots spilled into the streets.

Mouth wide with the sawing pull of his breath, grim with the danger that held him here motionless, he heard startled curses. "Christ — he got Jake!" A yell went up. "What'll his ol' woman say?" somebody grumbled through the mutter and spur scrape, the wary calling back and forth. It seemed incredible they could not hear the shaking clamor of his heart. He was afraid to move, even to twist his head around, lest the boards cry out under him or someone over on the other side or farther up or down the street, discover him.

Half strangled, Maffitt let go of his breath. They were scattering now, fanning out to comb the roundabout hide holes. Six of them anyway, maybe more. He was a little astonished the shot hadn't fetched some kind of law over here. He didn't catch Casas' voice, nor hardly expected to — not with that shot guy sprawled on the walk. He had really played into their hands, dropping that fellow. Casas would find some neat story to account for it; he might come right out into the open now.

Maffitt crouched there and sweated. There were warehouses over the stirred dust, a couple of stores not yet opened for trade. The buildings on this side — at least those around him — were mostly given over to small flats and offices. At the north end of this block were what had appeared to be several private residences, nothing very impressive; people of means lived on roads farther out.

They must know he couldn't have got far. Still, if any of them were thinkers they'd have had him already. The fools weren't even searching this building.

He began to breathe easier. So long as Casas didn't mix into this . . . But Casas would. He had almost nailed Maffitt south of the line. Maffitt wasn't building his hopes up. He was in a bad bind. He couldn't afford to move and he couldn't afford to remain where he was. Sooner or later someone down there would spot him. And all this while something had been gnawing at him, an intense disquiet. It had started with that clatter as he'd come over the rail, and that yell had confirmed it; he'd dropped his pistol getting onto this perch.

Slowly, with an extreme care, he twisted his neck. The lower half of the window behind him was open. From what little he could see the room looked to be lived in. There were tied-back drapes behind a mesh of lace curtains; he could just make out the brass of a bed post. If there was anyone in there . . .

Blobs of sweat dropped off the end of his nose.

He told himself if there'd been anyone in there those fellows down below would have been onto him straight off. But he was wrong about that.

"*When you leave,*" someone said, "*you'd better use the stairs.*"

2

A lot of things tramped through Maffitt's head in that moment none of them appearing to be of much help. The voice had come from the window — a woman's crisp, assured.

Every hair on the back of Maffitt's neck was up. *You never knew what a fool woman might do.* He itched to look into the street, didn't dare to. He got a crick in his neck from the awkward way he was holding it. All he needed by God, was to sneeze, he thought bitterly.

He said, cursing under his breath, "This your place, ma'am?"

"I live here. Anything else you'd like to know?"

Cool all right. Probably had a gun on him. More sweat ran down the channels of his face and he could feel the damp bind of it across his shoulders. He said, "Anyone looking up here?"

"I'm not about to come near enough to

19

see." She had the whip hand all right. She said, "You'd better get in here."

He was tempted. But Casas' bravos were still down there someplace. They might not be such fools as they'd seemed. They might even have him spotted, just waiting for him to get up and give them a better target.

"No, thanks," he grunted.

"You can't stay there until dark!"

"Why not?" Maffitt said. His neck was getting stiff. She was probably right but he'd play hell getting that horse to Bridle Bit if he rose up now and got himself shot.

Her tone became sharper. "They won't bother you here."

Maffitt couldn't make anything out of that, except if she were right she knew entirely too much about them. He wondered if one of those bastards just happened to be kin of hers? He didn't waste much thought on it. He'd obviously look a lot worse and be considerable more exposed getting down off this contraption than he would stepping into the room now he was up here. But he didn't trust her an inch. She was a heap too cool and too goddam interested. Like, by God, he might be leaving her his will!

"I can always scream, you know," she reminded him.

Maffitt swore out loud, but he got up and

20

climbed gingerly over the sill, turning at once to peer down at the street through the whorls of dropped curtain. He found nothing to alarm him, and this got his wind up more. The whole thing appeared too unlikely, every part of it; and pushing the curtain a little out with his hand, he bent to stare a long moment in the direction of Customs, discovering neither Casas nor any evidence of excitement.

He swung around then, facing her, catching dead-on the direct interest of her stare. She was backed against a dresser and he'd been right about the gun — both guns. His own was gone and hers, a two-barreled gambler's job, was competently focused.

She appeared tall for a woman and thin, but not too thin. Much younger than he'd imagined — too young for the hard core of knowledge exhibited by her carriage and actions. She revealed no embarrassment, only a collected, wary watchfulness more disturbing to Maffit than the threat of her pistol.

There was no possibility of any proper relationship between this girl and those thugs in the street; if she wasn't quite a lady at least she'd been given that kind of raising. The marks of this were plenty apparent. Her dress, pale blue and snugly fitted at waist and breast, made pleasing contrast with high-piled hair that looked the color of rust. Her eyes were a kind of deep-shining brown almost golden, alert yet quiet with a depth of perception beyond her years. These things, uncomfortably nagging him, were fuel to Maffitt's increasing resentment.

He knew how he looked without a shave in three days, grimy with trail dust and stinking of sweat. She had a short upper lip and a full lower one and both of them showing too red in this light and beginning to twitch in the tug of a smile. He made no effort to conceal his irritation.

Color touched her cheeks and turned them scornful. "It doesn't matter what you think of me —"

"You're wasting your time," Maffitt said, "and it always does to a woman. Where's the stairs?"

Her glance sharpened angrily. She struck back at once. "I saw you kill that man. What have you done with the gun?"

Maffitt's jaws locked tight. He saw a door beyond the bed but before he could move she'd stepped into his path. "No one will blame me if you happen to get shot."

Maffitt, shrugging, settled into his tracks. She looked perfectly capable of carrying out the threat. He was angry, suddenly and deeply and he had no further scruples.

"The gun," she said.

"I lost it getting up there."

She stepped around the bed, putting it between them, amusing at the balked look of him. "You might as well make yourself comfortable." She indicated a platform rocker a couple of yards beyond his clenched fist. "They've probably found the gun. In any event we're stuck here till dark."

Maffitt said bluntly, "What do you want of me?"

"All I want is to get away from here."

He studied the cool composure of her face, considering the unsaid things her words implied, more and more disturbed, more bitterly distrustful, resenting her advantages, the steady muzzles of that pistol and the proximity of Casas' hirelings which put him in her power.

He said at last, "The town's full of horses. If you've got to have help —"

"I don't want that kind." She had the grace to blush but her measuring glance never left his face. "I need a man who hasn't got time for any foolishness."

Maffitt's stubbled cheeks darkened. "You don't know anything about me."

"I know enough to get you hanged or shot."

She met the hard rage of his stare without blinking. They crossed wills through a lengthening stillness. Her glance never wavered, she was impenetrably wrapped in the armor of her knowledge. He finally said, "I guess you know what you want," and dropped into the rocker.

She dug up a confident nod. "We understand each other. You will take my orders for as long as you have to. Now, I suppose you're hungry. Do I have your word you'll behave for the moment?"

Maffitt stared at her bleakly.

"You don't have much choice," she said, watching him out of the corners of her eyes. She laid her gun on the dresser, swung around and pulled open the door. "There's a bottle under the bed. I'll go fix something to eat." She glanced toward the window, flashing her eyes at him and left.

He stared at the gun. He could hear her moving around, commencing supper sounds. She hadn't closed the door but she was out of his sight. He got up and found the bottle and taking a stiff pull, stood behind the curtain glaring down into the sun drenched empty street. A good grade of whisky. He could feel the creep and bite of it but his problems remained sharply with him.

No point getting back on that balcony. He could likely overpower her now she'd put aside the pistol, but not before she'd fetched Casas' thugs. One yell and they'd come swarming. He thrust the bottle back under the bed and came impatiently up and then dropped into the chair.

He was boxed and bitter, tired and depressed from hours in the saddle and longer hours under that cottonwood's branches and too much beating of his head against the rocks. He was weary clean through . . . of lonely nights and futile regrets, of specters and phantoms and the ghosts of lost chances, of shifts and dodges and the prowl of strange faces and the increasing strain of unremitting vigilance. He was fed to the gills with violence and flight, of waking in strange places with no roots in routine except the constant need of holding himself in readiness either to run or to shoot when flight was denied and he stood trapped . . . as he was now.

He had thought to be done with running when he'd made up his mind to go home. But he'd found the Old Man dead with nothing left but debts — absorbed by Breeding to keep the ranch intact. There'd been nothing to get his teeth into and the stake dangled in front of him by Breeding's offer had looked almighty good.

Now he wasn't so sure. A lot of doubts had been stirred in these last few days and he was wondering if Breeding hadn't taken this means of ridding himself of an unwanted presence. Breeding knew the Maffitts had long been fools about horses.

The Old Man at one time had figured to raise remounts and had put together a pretty fair stud but with the decline of Indian troubles the garrisons had been disbanded and the dream had petered out. The only horses Breeding had ever given two hoots about were those that could get up and go on a race strip. After he'd bought into the ranch most of the horse stock was turned into bangtails. Bridle Bit had achieved no little fame in this direction. Breeding was a good judge of sprinters, whisky and other men's weaknesses. He'd likely wanted this horse but, knowing about Afligido, wasn't it more than a little bit probable he might also have known more about Olivares than he'd seen fit to mention?

Well, Breeding would keep. If there was any hokus pokus behind this Bridle Bit freeze-out he would uncover it when he got back there. When, that is, and if.

He looked over the room trying to find

some clue to the identity or character of the man who was footing the bills for this filly. It was a girl's room with nothing masculine in it but the pistol and the bottle cached under the bed. A man was pretty far gone when his women had to hide it.

No rings on her fingers, but that didn't prove much. Come right down to it there was no proof she lived here, only her word for it. Maffitt swore under his breath. Too bad questions wasn't dollars! But one thing he was sure of: Him and this willful was splitting their tracks at the first halfway chance he got hold of!

In Maffitt's experience there were two kinds of women and it angered him to find this girl unsettling his judgment. Her actions and the look of her just plain wouldn't gee. She had a damn inviting mouth. There was rouge on her lips and too much wisdom in the cut of her whip-sharp eyes. Cool as a well chain, quick and ready, but she carried herself like a thoroughbred. She didn't talk like trash and she didn't look like trash either.

"All right," she called, "come and get it."

Maffitt tramped through the door and found himself in a kitchen. If this was a woman turning bad she'd found a smart way to do it. He saw a pail and dipper on the wooden drainboard of a sink; soap lay beside it with a towel and an agateware basin. Maffitt went over and splashed water on himself. He rubbed the dirt off on the towel and heat curled around him with its fragrance of food and he heard her light step going from stove to table. If they were stopped or caught up with he wouldn't get much chance to make himself heard — not, he thought dourly, that anyone would believe him. She still had on the blue dress. He said, scowling at it, "You fixing to go in that?"

She had a sultry way of sliding her eyes around and used this now, hiding the laughter he sensed inside her. "I have to think of appearances."

"Appear— by God! You got any idea what that brush is?"

"There won't be much brush the way we'll be taking." There was a faint beading of moisture on her upper lip and the heat from the stove had put more color in her face. "I'll be picking the trail. I know this country a lot better than you do."

Maffitt opened his mouth but shut his teeth without speaking.

Her eyes watched him calmly. "Just before daylight you crossed the border on a horse — don't bother lying. I happened to see you. Then you dropped out of sight. This evening you turn up without the horse. I hope you've got it handy. When you get in trouble with Casas a horse is the handiest thing a man can hope to get his hands on."

They watched each other through a deepening silence. At last Maffitt said, "How'd you know it was Casas?"

"I recognized one of his men out there. That fat-faced fellow with the scar along his jaw. They call him Rubio."

"For a lady," Maffitt said, "you've got —"

"There's nothing mysterious about it." She waved a hand. "Better pull up a chair before this meal gets cold. We'll be moving before long and I've still got to fix some kind of snack to tide us over; we'd best keep away from towns till we get deep into Texas."

Maffitt said, "I'm not headed for Texas."

A shadow crossed her face and then, alert again, she nodded. "Don't you imagine Casas knows that?"

It stopped him cold. This wasn't any spur of the moment impulse on her part. She'd got it all doped out, knew exactly what she was doing. She said, watching him gravely, "Did you steal the horse?"

Maffitt, still scowling, sat gingerly down on an edge of the chair. He dug out his bill of sale and tossed it across the table. She fetched up her own chair, glanced at the paper and passed it back. She said, "They wouldn't sell Afligido for that price — they did, of course, but nobody'd ever believe it. See where that leaves you? They will deny ever seeing that paper. All you've got is a signature that might very well have been forged."

"Why'd he bother to hire thugs if —"

"Quicker and cheaper. It doesn't embarrass the General."

Maffitt tied into his grub, chomping angrily. The girl took up her fork. "You were luckier than you know when you picked our porch to climb up on. And you were luckier still when you ran into me." She said, smiling a little, "I might not have been here." She considered her plate. "We were both lucky, I guess." Her eyes came up again then, darkly watching him. "I think," she said tentatively, "we'll be good for each other."

Maffitt kept on with his eating, face inscrutable.

There was a hint of softness in the rounded contours of her lower lip, of invitation almost. Maffitt, lifting hard eyes, said suddenly, "You're not living here alone."

She appeared a little surprised and then amused. "My father pays the rent." She

30

looked at him quizzically. "I'm Katherin Barr . . ."

Something, far back in Maffitt's head, stirred uneasily; but he couldn't haul it into the light, couldn't even be certain the name had any connection. "Where is he now?"

"Bisbee, probably. He's away a great deal."

She was watching Maffitt, fork lowered, her weighing glance a little darker and more searching as though she might at this late moment be wondering if she had been as smart as she had figured in attempting to coerce and control so grim a man. His eyes met hers and something she must have read in them released her breath. She said, suddenly smiling, "What do I call you?"

"Maffitt's my name. Dale Maffitt."

Obviously the name meant nothing to her. "Well, Maffitt," she said, getting up, "if you'll excuse me I'll start throwing together —"

"How old are you?"

Color came into her cheeks. "Old enough to know what I'm doing."

"Then you're a fool," he said, and went on with his eating.

The tone of it whipped her around, tight with anger. "You don't know anything about what I have to put up with!"

"You're not starvin'," he said through the mouthful he was chewing. "You ain't been knocked around much. If you had half the sense you was born with —"

"You're not getting rid of me that easy." Her red mouth curled. "You're not leaving unless I leave with you. You can make up your mind to that right now!"

3

It was still not quite dark when she handed him the pistol — not the belly gun she'd first stuck him up with but an improved Army model Remington, .44-40 calibre, with an eight-inch octagon barrel; a five-shot, fully loaded. He could see the brass shine of the cartridge rims and thought of the man he'd left dead on the walk. He got up off the bed and stashed the pistol in the belt band of his pants without comment, smelling the thin film of gun oil. She said, "Can you get these sandwiches into your pockets?"

He nodded. Smart. Not careless enough to leave the house carrying things. "But you'll need a hat." He scooped up his own. "That sun by tomorrow noon —"

"If we waited till dark I could wear one. They're going to see us leave anyway. Better if they think we're just walking around." She went and stared through the window. "If it was full dark they'd follow us." She said then, cryptically, "Casas can't afford any more mistakes on this side."

Maffitt shrugged. In his own mind he was pretty well convinced the big Mexican wouldn't let them out of his sight. "I don't like this," he growled as they crept down the stairs. "What they can see they can drive a knife into."

"We can't wait any longer." She didn't look around at him. "Where is that horse?"

Maffitt said grudgingly, "In the government stables," and saw the whole length of her stiffen. She did look back now. In the heavy gloom of this covered stairway her eyes were like bright shards of glass. Thinking of how this affected her own schemes. He saw the deep breath she pulled into her.

"You left Afligido with the Border Patrol horses!"

By her tone she might have said, *You've cut both of our throats.* There was a stunned incredulity in the brittleness of those words that pulled a chuckle out of Maffitt. "Seemed like a pretty slick notion — I didn't have much time to go prospecting around."

"But how will you get him?"

"I'll get him," Maffitt growled. "What're you doing for a mount? I can walk through

Customs and reach Afligido. But if they're watching you too and you go to a stable —"

"I'll get a horse off the street."

Maffitt looked at her. "Lovely!" he said, disgusted. "And if we're caught I'll get strung up for it."

"Then you'd better not be caught." She went on down the stairs. There was no door at the bottom. Just inside the entrance she waited. "Take my arm."

"Might be better if you weren't so close to me."

"You'd better be glad I am close to you. You wouldn't get ten steps from here by yourself. You wouldn't get Afligido loose, either. Being well known in this town is one of the crosses I've had to bear. It will work in your favor."

Maffitt tramped the first fifty feet in the completest kind of silence. She probably sensed his irritation. "Relax," she said crisp as cabbage leaves. "You're not walking on eggs. Talk to me. Act like you're enjoying yourself."

Light from Customs showed the glint of his teeth. "It's damn plain," he said, "that you are!"

A laugh fell out of her, gay, half shy, and she hugged his arm to her, looking up into his face for all the world like a moonstruck kid. A cool and willful lot, he thought grimly, giving these accomplishments a grudging admiration that in no way lessened the grip of his outrage. She saw the wild fury and quickened her step. "I'm not going to run," he growled.

"I know, but I'm not sure you do." She let go of him though when they came full into the brightness around Customs.

"You better be lookin' around for a horse."

She paid no attention. She was tense, staring past him. Following her look he saw a man cutting toward them from a thickness of shadows along the opposite side. This fellow was tall like the jaws of a wolf trap in white pantalones with a bright touch of red around his waist — Chico Casas!

Maffitt's mouth tightened. The girl was rooted with shock. There was no place to run even if he'd been minded to. They were full in the lights of the barricade; there were uniformed men on both sides of the Line.

Casas came up, doffing his hat with a flourish. "Miss Barr! How good to see you!" He grinned widely, bold eyes ogling the curves of her figure. He captured her hand, bending over it with an effusive gallantry. One would never have guessed the two men were acquainted, the enquiring way Casas' eyes played over Maffitt as he straightened.

Katherin said, "You're looking fit, Chico," and then more formally, "Colonel, I'd like to have you know one of father's oldest friends, Dale Maffitt — Colonel Casas."

If Casas was disquieted by her lie he did not show it. His smile reached out enfolding Maffitt warmly. "Any friend of Sheriff Barr would always have my completest endorsement," he said heartily, but it was noticeable neither hand made any move in Maffitt's direction.

Maffitt didn't say anything at all. He was caught in the bitter jolt the Mexican's revelation of her father's business had given him. A sheriff!

Katherin said, taking Maffitt's arm, "I'm afraid we will have to go. It's been nice seeing you, Chico, but the Captain will be neck deep in a stew if we keep him waiting much longer."

She steered Maffitt into the building, through the counterlined lobby and down a short hallway that was banked with the cubbyholes of petty officials. One door, standing open, was labeled BORDER PATROL — Captain E. K. Bless. The room was lighted but empty. The girl turned into it, taking Maffitt with her — "Just in case Chico's watching," she said, thin lipped with strain. There was another door across the room between the desk and a filing cabinet; she pushed Maffitt hurriedly toward it. "It goes down a runway that comes out at the stables — hurry!" she said, almost stepping on his heels.

It occurred to Maffitt that Casas, if the man knew of this passage, might very well arrive at the same destination; but mostly Maffitt's confusion of thoughts as they hurried down the dim lane had to do with the imagined reactions of Sheriff Barr when that officer discovered his daughter had gone off with some saddle bum. *Disappeared* was the way the man would probably phrase it — there'd be no hurdle at all from that to *abducted.*

Maffitt was in a fine sweat by the time they reached the stables. The last thing he wanted was to have the law after him — that was one thing he'd stayed clear of. A side door was just in front of them when Katherin said, "If Chico was watching I hope he's still at it," and shivered. Maffitt was too filled with his own thoughts to wonder. When he realized she'd spoken he said, "You'd better get back and start hunting that mount," but, reaching ahead of him, she pulled open the door.

There was a group of khaki-clad men

about a huddle of lanterns, and inside this huddle Maffitt saw the dark head of Afligido. "Well, fat's in the fire," Katherin muttered, and went forward.

Their steps were heard and several heads came around. Afligido nickered. A short heavy-set mustached man with a captain's insignia on his shirt collar stepped out of the group with a surprised smile for the girl and a sharp look at Maffitt. The girl said coolly, "That horse belongs to this man, Captain — I came along to make sure there's no trouble about it."

Bless looked at them curiously, first at the girl, then at Maffitt and, rather thoughtfully, back again. "Nice looking animal," he observed noncommittally. His glance took in Maffitt's brush-clawed clothes and stubbled cheeks. "A long way from home."

It wasn't entirely clear whether he referred to the horse or Maffitt. Katherin made the introdutions. "An old friend of Dad's."

"Squabble O," Bless said, "that's Olivares." His eyes were blunt. "This horse hasn't been through Customs."

Katherin dredged up a smile. "Dale didn't have time. He ran into a bunch of bandits coming out of those mountains. For a while there, I guess, it was nip and tuck."

"Mostly nip," Maffitt put in, figuring he'd better say something.

Bless looked pretty grim. "Feller got killed here in town this evening." They were all watching Maffitt. "You reckon that could have been one of them?"

He was nobody's fool.

Maffitt said with a shrug, "Don't seem too likely they'd have hung around that long. I lost them over there near that bull ring — got across before dawn. Been under cover all day."

"He's been at our place."

"The body was found not far from your house. Seems to have been quite a commotion." Bless' eyes, stabbing Maffitt swung around to the girl. "How did the horse come to be in these stables?"

Her smile was disarming. "Dale couldn't think of a safer place. Had to leave him somewhere while he came on to find Dad. Said he'd square with you later; that's what we've come for."

"The horse," Bless said, "will have to be cleared through Customs."

Katherin's brows went up. "Ernie, don't be stuffy! You know very well you can take care of it." The captain frowned uncomfortably. "This is sheriff's business," the girl pressed. "Dad's waiting for Dale at Here-

40

ford right now. We've got to get over there."

"When I found he'd gone on I wouldn't have stopped," Maffitt said, "but Miss Barr was afraid that crowd was still after me."

Bless was plainly uneasy and even halfway suspicious as, of course, he had every right to be. Maffitt should not have come here looking like a brush jumper but he hadn't expected to run into the captain or to have Katherin with him. He said, hoping to put a better face on things (like his lack of a shave with all day on his hands), "I've been keeping my eyes peeled. If there's any of that bunch around I haven't seen them. Still and all, there's some risk; I don't think Miss Barr ought to go —"

"Nonsense!" Katherin said sharply. "If that gang is still hunting you it would be crazy to stick to the roads, and you don't know this back country like I do. I can get you through — we've been over all this!" She turned her glance back on Bless. "Dad's counting on having the horse there tonight."

Afligido was impatient, too, stamping and blowing like the deer flies were at him. The captain was on a spot with those troopers standing around taking this in. A pair of them, back of him, looking from Bless to the girl, were openly grinning. Was Bless one of the reasons she had to get away?

41

The captain said, trying to conceal his annoyance, "What evidence do you have to establish your right to the horse?"

Maffitt, with some misgivings, got out the bill of sale he'd shown Katherin. Bless pounced on the same pair of weaknesses the girl had. "That's a pretty cheap price for a horse of this caliber." He regarded Maffitt inscrutably. "That scrawl of Olivares' could be approximated almost by anyone. Do you have anything else?"

Maffitt, keeping hold of his temper, shook his head. But Katherin cried angrily, "I told you he was acting for the sheriff's office —"

"The sheriff isn't here," Bless said stubbornly, "and I can't for the life of me see —"

"Casas is in town." The girl said scornfully, "If you won't take Dale's word or mine, get him over here. He can verify the signature."

Maffitt, locked in his tracks, scarcely daring to breathe, was appalled to hear himself saying, "That's right. He was there. He'll know all about it."

Bless, still eyeing the girl, slapped a hand out, giving way with what grace he was able to manage. "Ryan, saddle the horse." His cheeks came about and his eyes, touching Maffitt, were a wholly noncommittal gray.

He handed back the bill of sale. "Good

riding," he growled with the grimmest of nods. Then he paused to add dryly, "You are fortunate in having so able a talent as Miss Barr's. I've no doubt she'll get you through. If you'll excuse me now . . ." Giving Maffitt another bleak look he was about to turn away when Katherin said, "Ernie, you'll have to lend me a horse."

Bless, cheeks flushed with the severity of his emotions, gave the order. Jerking a final curt nod he departed through the door opening into the bypass which led back to his office.

4

Maffitt hadn't imagined anyone in such circumstances could get clear of Naco without being discovered. It was not a large place. There was open country all around. The sparse brush lifting over the rolling ground hereabouts came no higher than Afligido's shoulders. Expecting trouble — even angrily looking forward to it as a possible means of shaking free of the girl — he'd been counting on Afligido's proven speed to pull him clear. But Katherin got him away from the town as neatly and quietly as though she'd been doing such things all her life.

Through the sounds of their walking horses she murmured, "No point trying to lay a false trail. Distance is the only thing now that can help us."

Maffitt was willing to subscribe to that. Casas was not going to be fooled for very long. And that captain! Was he one of the reasons the girl was doing this crazy thing?

44

The fellow had certainly gone more than out of his way to oblige her and, just as surely, hadn't liked it. The more Bless poked this business around the more dissatisfied he was likely to become. Sooner or later the man was going to dig into it.

After paying duty on the horse Maffitt was practically strapped. He had no more than three or four dollars in his pockets. On his own this wouldn't have bothered him a particle; it was the girl who unsettled and played hob with every prospect.

Bless probably would stew and fume until her father got back and discovered Katherin gone. The captain's own feelings when that happened would doubtless bring him to the same views arrived at by the sheriff. The whole country would be alerted. Every jasper in miles would be after Dale then and it would be dead or alive, with all the odds on the former.

Swearing about it wasn't going to change anything. For several miles Maffitt considered running away from her. On Afligido he could probably do it no matter how well Bless had mounted her. These government horses weren't culls but they sure as hell weren't race horses. Maffitt told himself he didn't owe her a thing.

He was wildly furious — almost savagely

so. He'd spent the biggest portion of his twenty-seven years avoiding every chance of even remotely becoming responsible for anything and here he was, saddled with a woman! Whipped, not by the things other people might say, but the country itself — its deceptiveness, its very vastness, these arid leagues on leagues of indescribable desolation and the prowlers who drifted like gray ghosts across it.

They rode steadily, walk and trot and walk again, mile after mile through the night's covering darkness. There was no moon. Not many stars got through the highflung rack of clouds above them, yet not once did the girl appear in doubt of their direction. This, too, contributed to Maffitt's unsettled temper. She was entirely too sure of herself, and of him. She rode in the lead and never once looked around.

At least, he thought irascibly, she wasn't one to talk a man's arm off. Nobody was going to do much tracking before dawn but with the first light of day Casas and his bravos were going to be hard after them — unless, he thought, suddenly stiffening, Casas got it out of Bless where they were bound for. Casas, increasingly impatient, might have gone into the building after them; Afligido would be reason enough if he wanted to claim the horse had been stolen.

Bless, of course, might deny any knowledge of their whereabouts, or of Maffitt. He might, on the other hand, admit the girl had set off for Hereford. Casas had seen them together, probably knew she'd been hiding him. If Bless revealed the destination she had given, Maffitt did not think Casas would be deluded into going there; he'd be more apt to split his crew, staying with part of them to pick up Maffitt's trail in the morning. He would know the black horse's tracks.

This would give them about an eight hour lead but Casas, unless they made some effort to hide their trail, would cut that down in a hurry. "We going to cross any streams?" Maffitt finally asked.

"Not tonight," Katherin said, and went back to her thoughts.

Toward morning she swung sharply away from the course they'd been following. She didn't offer any explanation and Maffitt rode dourly after her, holding his tongue but unable to curb the disquieting suspicions that began to nag and prod him. Back at the house she had said they would make directly for Texas, implying such a move would not be looked for by Casas; and he'd been willing to concede this much. So why was she suddenly pointing into the north? To avoid Douglas? They should already have passed Douglas some while ago; there was no reason to believe they hadn't. Maffitt had seen scattered lights and there was no other town of any size on the line she had taken but Paso del Norte which they never could have reached in one night's ride — or in two, for that matter. Between here and there, and not too far beyond Douglas, they'd be into New Mexico.

They might even be now.

He still couldn't satisfactorily account for the switch. The shortest way into Texas from Naco was east by northeast. Or you could head straight east and, by adding another hundred miles to the trip, get into it through Mexico. In fact you'd have to cross pretty near a hundred miles of mañana land regardless unless you were prepared to skirt a right angle which would pile up extra mileage into almost double that amount. Was that what she was doing? Attempting to avoid this Mexican gallop? Or was there a man somewhere waiting for her? Some hombre her father had forbidden her to see?

This made sense, and Maffitt assured himself he truly hoped it were so. He'd be rid of her then in good conscience; left again to his own devices. This would suit him right down to the ground and should have raised his spirits considerably.

But something about the notion turned him fidgety, depressing him. He wouldn't let himself dig into this reaction, choosing instead to think of Casas, and wondering if the man with Mexican ingenuity had someway managed to divine their destination, was perhaps even now leading his hirelings by some short cut to head them off.

It wasn't likely. The girl had claimed to know this country and certainly she had acted the part. If there'd been any short cuts she'd have taken them; maybe here was the reason she'd so suddenly swung north.

He looked around, attempting to find some basis for this. They were gradually climbing and appeared to be traversing some kind of shallow canyon that was filled with broken rocks and ran to catclaw, soapweed and cholla. He saw no sign of any trail yet there must have been one, the girl was never at a loss for direction.

The shadows were beginning to pale when they came into a long and wide level where thick and cured grass changed the sound of the hoofs. Eastward the overhead was definitely lighter where it met the jumbled tops of a low line of ragged hills. Northward a desert threw off its dim shine, and now the girl swung east again and presently they were rising from one hogback to another until Maffitt in a sweat of protest finally growled, "This is a damn good way to get ourselves seen."

She looked around at him then and threw up a hand pointing back of him southwestward. Apparently they'd been skirting a mountain mass whose existence he hadn't suspected. "They're not going to see very much through that. They probably haven't even got started yet."

She creaked around in her saddle and sent her horse on. She made a straight slim shape against the increasing light in the east. No sag to those shoulders though she must be feeling these long hours just as he was. No complaints.

He hauled up on that thought. Of course she wasn't complaining — she was doing what she wanted to do, otherwise she wouldn't be out here. A fool just the same. Any woman was who gave up her home to run off with some man she had never before heard of! The worst kind of fool, Maffitt told himself disgustedly.

Around here they hanged men caught stealing horses; were they like to do less for a son of a bitch who ran off with a girl?

He started sweating all over. He thought

again, too, of cutting loose from her, right here. Resentment mostly, the need to blow off steam, because he knew damn well he wasn't about to do it.

Twenty minutes later they came out of a draw and ahead there was a huddle of unpainted shacks. These were set down squarely in the middle of a basin.

The girl drew rein and Maffitt glanced at her inquiringly.

"McQuirchee's Wells," she said with a sigh. She got out of the saddle and, stripping off the horse's bridle, turned him loose so he could graze. "We may as well eat that stuff before it spoils."

Maffitt, watching her stamping around, stretching her legs, thought that damned dress about as unlikely as she could have picked for this trip. "How're we going to get around that place?" He studied the basin with a dissatisfied stare. No trees, no brush tall enough to hide a coyote. "If we're seen we'll be remembered."

He scowled at the dress again, suddenly hating it.

She glanced down at the expensive material and tried to rub out some of the wrinkles. Her glance lifted. "I'm counting on it."

"Counting — !" He looked as though she'd gone straight off her rocker.

"Why else would I have put on so conspic-uous a dress?" She showed her impatience. "Did you suppose we'd come up here to avoid being seen? I *want* to be seen — I want *both* of us to be. There was no point at all going out of our way if we're not going to be remembered."

Maffitt felt like hitting her. All his outrage came up into his throat and the bent blunt fingers of his big-knuckled hands looked as though for two cents they would rip the dress off her.

She went back half a step, mouth sprung open. He almost did hit her then. It was her eyes, he guessed, that kept his hands off her; even big with shock they never left his face.

He flexed burly shoulders with a kind of snarl, jerked the sandwiches out of his pockets and hurled them down on the ground like they were snakes. He slammed into the saddle and was lifting the reins when Katherin cried sharply: "Wait!"

He heard her high-heeled slippers making tough going of the sand, felt her hand on his leg and glared down at her intolerably. She was flushed, breathing hard. Dust was smeared across the bridge of her nose. She looked up at him. "It was all for you —"

"For me!" He laughed bitterly, angrily tightening his grip on the reins. The bay sidestepped nervously, flattening his ears. The girl, keeping hold of Maffitt, paid Afligido no attention. "For your own protection — you've got to listen! It's all I've thought about all night. McQuirchee's a justice of the peace. He'll marry —"

"By God! You *are* loco!"

"But don't you see?" she cried — "if we're married they can't touch you!"

Maffitt stared a long time. Color came and turned her cheeks blotchy while he held Afligido forgotten on the reins.

"It — it wouldn't mean anything . . . when we're clear I'd let you go." A sudden dark flashed through her look. "You're not already married are you?"

Maffitt said bitterly, "Would that make any difference?"

"I guess not." Her eyes dropped.

He was caught in emotions too powerful to sort. This was madness, but she did have a head on her. It wouldn't stop Casas but it would tie Bless' hands and her father's besides. Well — maybe not her father's. If Barr were stubborn enough, or furious enough, he might prefer to see Katherin a widow. It ought anyway to prevent him putting a price on Maffitt's hide.

But all the suspicions were at work in him again. This could be another trap, a more solid way of tying him to her, of making him responsible. Making sure he didn't run out.

He did not shrug the thought away but held it gingerly in a kind of suspension. The big facts were still in front of him. He was no more anxious to be dead than the next man. "All right," he said, "let's get it over."

She loosed a long sigh and let go of him. She went over and picked up the sandwiches, even the pair that had burst out of their papers. She came back, reaching out to him the lion's share.

"No time for that now," he growled, plainly impatient. She looked more chipper, almost smiling, now that she'd got her way. It did not improve his temper to notice she'd held back the dirtied food for herself. "Fork your bronc and let's get this over with."

She peered up at him, sobering. She finally said meekly, "Can't we wait for the sun? I know you're anxious to be on your way but some of these people might not be up. Wouldn't it be better to have them *all* in on this?"

Maffitt, scowling, considered her mount. Both animals could do with a rest and some grain.

"There's a creek," she said, "just a bit east of here."

He caught her thought. They could use

the creek to confuse their trail; it might get back some of the time lost here. He got grudgingly down, grabbed the dirtied food and commenced chewing into it. "Better walk that horse around some while you're eatin'."

Ten minutes after the sun pushed its butter-yellow light across those eastern crags they were riding their horses into McQuirchee's yard. Dogs ran yapping about their heels and a couple of naked mixed-blood toddlers stared curiously at them from a cavelike burrow in a discolored mound of last year's hay.

Wood smoke carried its biting tang across the hoof-pocked plaza and a dark-faced breed unwinkingly eyed them from the door of a shack. Three fellows in cowpuncher garb readying mounts to the left of the central corral twisted around to stare, and a thickset man in galluses sweeping off the store's porch shaded his eyes and growled some uncaught remark through the open door behind him.

"You'd better do the talking," she said, tugging down her skirts as though abruptly conscious of the general interest. A gust of color swirled into her cheeks and Maffitt observing this, guessed she was probably regretting throwing away those torn stockings.

A man's long and stooped shape came out of the store's door hole, taking a quick look from a pair of squinched eyes that were the shade of wet ashes. He was hound-dog thin. A cud of tobacco big as a pullet egg bulged out his left cheek, giving the whole look of him an off-center slant. He had on no shirt. His rib-rutted torso was encased in the top half of a pair of long handles whose once fire-red hue was faded pink across the shoulders. He had his legs thrust into a pair of grimy Texas pants made of rust colored canvas. A shell belt and dark-butted pistol were strapped about his hipless middle and his hair, a brindled sorrel, was shaggy as a collie pup's.

"Howdy," he said, straightening up to spit. He showed rotten teeth in a gargoyle grin as his eyes reached over to take hold of the girl. "You 'uns musta got up before breakfast."

"I'm looking for McQuirchee," Maffitt said.

"Wal, you won't hev far to hunt. Light down an' rest your calluses." The man unloaded another mouthful of juice. "You figgerin' to get them hawses fed?"

"Grained."

"You come to the right place — tend to it," Brindle Hair said, waving the breed over.

His lecherous stare inspected Katherin again. "What's to be your pleasure, folks? Hot meal or a marryin'?" His glance quartered over the dun distance behind them. "No dust. You musta got a good start —"

"No one asked for your opinion."

McQuirchee, mean eyes narrowing, rubbed a hand over his leg about three inches from the sweat-darkened grips of his pistol. Maffitt showed no concern. "Little techy ain't you?" McQuirchee laughed, and covered the bluster with a show of bluff heartiness, saying, "Come in, come in," when Maffitt's look didn't change.

Maffitt swung down, handing Afligido's reins to the waiting breed. The girl, with a heated look at those still interested men taking all of this in from their stance by the corrals, showed her legs again as she came out of the saddle. Head high she followed Maffitt into the store.

McQuirchee sat on a counter beside a pile of blankets. "If it's a marryin'," he said, "we're gonna hev to hev witnesses. You got a license? . . . Wal, no matter," he grinned, taking his answer from Maffitt's look. "I kin fix jest about anythin' — for a price."

Maffitt fingered the three cartwheels and the four-bit piece which was all he had left to jingle in his pockets. "How much is this going to cost me?"

"Don't git up no lather over that," the trader said and, stepping to the door, sent out a call for witnesses. "I tie 'em tighter'n a bull's ass," he declared with a leer at the girl's tight-cheeked face, "an' price don't enter into it. But of course," he added with a calculating grin, "no man would hanker to make a cheap show in front of so high-steppin' a filly as this 'un."

"I've got three dollars and fifty cents," Maffitt said, and put it down on the counter.

"That's all right. I'll give you somethin' on that horse."

"The horse isn't marrying her."

All the jocularity dropped out of the trader's face. "Must think more of that black than you do of your woman."

"Three fifty," Maffitt said.

McQuirchee spat. "That'll jest about cover the grain he's et." Scooping up the money he dropped it into a greasy purse. Booted feet rumbled up the steps of the porch.

Katherin said, "How much will it be?"

The man, scratching himself, regarded her dubiously, finally prodding up a grin. "Fer you, little lady, it'll be just ten bucks." His eyes sharpened with interest as her hand disappeared inside the front of her dress.

58

She turned away from him then. After a series of adjustments she walked over to the counter and laid down two five dollar bills.

McQuirchee scowled. "That the best you kin do?"

"It's what you asked for, isn't it?"

"What I meant was hard money." He considered her shrewdly. "Iff'n you've got to give paper that'll be another five."

Biting her lip Katherin again turned away. Coming back to the counter she put down another bill. McQuirchee smirked. Shoving them into his pocket he told her, "You won't keep no man by payin' his way."

Maffitt, cheeks inscrutable, offered no comment.

The cowpunchers filed in. They got their backs to a wall, thumbs hooked over the rims of their shell belts. McQuirchee got a dog-eared book from behind the counter, again settled himself and said to Maffitt, "You got a ring?"

"I've got it," Katherin said, and dropped a plain gold band into the trader's grubby palm. McQuirchee caught the feel of Maffitt's glance and pulled his lip down.

The ceremony took five minutes. The certificate, filled out, McQuirchee put in Katherin's hands. Clearing the phlegm from his windpipe he said, "Tain't often around yere a feller gits t' tech tasters with anythin' so —" Colliding with Maffitt's stare he went still. A clock somewhere pushed solemn seconds across the interval. McQuirchee's mouth twisted meanly into a kind of sour grin and he said too loudly, "But seein' you folks is in sech a all-fired rush I'll take it out in watchin' the groom."

Maffitt jerked a stiff-cheeked nod toward the door. The girl walked past him. Before her heels reached the porch McQuirchee said, watching Maffitt, "Looks like too good of a hawss t' be packin' a saddle bum around through the cactus. Reckon you better stick right yere fer a spell. Onless, of course, you got proof?"

Maffitt, eyeing the hard-faced trio in puncher garb, knew this wasn't a time to get crusty. Reaching lefthandedly into his pocket he got out the bill of sale he'd shown Katherin. He held this out to the nearest of the three. The fellow glanced at it, shrugged, and passed it along. When it got to the trader, McQuirchee, without ever taking his eyes off Maffitt, tore it up. With a laugh he said, "Boys, it looks powerful like we've cotched ourselfs a hawss thief."

5

Maffitt's lips squeezed together. He looked pretty formidable, but so did the odds. The prolonged attention of his narrowed stare made no discernible dent on the trader. The man still held to his place on the counter with the flats of both hands gently pressed to its edge. He was sure of himself, sure he had Maffitt boxed.

"Of course," he said, chuckling, "I'm open to argufyin'."

The girl, half turned, tightly spoke from the doorway. "Do you know who I am?"

McQuirchee, still openly gloating, still sneering said, "Nope. An' care less."

"How much do you —"

"Katherin," Maffitt said, "keep out of this."

Even in the shadow of his floppy brimmed hat Maffitt's face showed greasy slick. He got out the makings, twisting up a smoke. "Not very good weather for dyin'," he said mildly.

McQuirchee grinned.

No one had to tell Maffitt he was caught where the hair was short. This post of McQuirchee's was an isolated place. Within reason the man could do just about anything he put his mind to. He had already decided Maffitt was on the run; nothing Maffitt could say was going to change this fellow's thinking. He was at home around here and Maffitt was a stranger with an obviously valuable stallion and a pretty little filly. McQuirchee's intentions were plenty apparent.

Nothing Maffitt had would be taken in trade for Afligido. The man already had the horse. He'd keep the girl until he got tired of her. Whoever was trailing Maffitt wasn't worrying McQuirchee a particle; he'd wave the pursuit right on. They would follow the tracks of Afligido and the girl's horse until they became lost someplace in the rocks a long way from here — like the truth of Maffitt's dying and the last days of this girl.

It was incredible and yet both possible and plausible. People were always disappearing in this kind of country; this was what he and Katherin had set out to do. No one was going to pin anything on McQuirchee.

"Your three guns," Maffitt said, "can probably take care of me, but what's going to happen to you while they're doing it?"

McQuirchee chuckled. "Any time you're ready go ahead an' we'll see."

"Maffitt," the girl gasped. Remembering the breed he understood McQuirchee's assurance. The breed would be crouched in the door now, shielded by Katherin's body.

Probably use a knife.

Anger surged like a miasmic black fog through the corridors of Maffitt's mind. Once again he was being pressured, forced into a crack that was not of his making, faced with violence and hate and all too probably death. He was filled with rebellion, trying to find a way out, some means of bypassing the responsibility with which the girl had saddled him — and could not.

He could feel the shakes getting into his legs. All the muscles of his stomach were knotted. Sweat glued the shirt to the backs of his shoulders. Without ever lifting his stare from McQuirchee he attempted to evaluate the three who were flanking him, trying to hunt out their weaknesses, their probable reactions and worth to the trader in terms of fire power; and all the while his skin was acrawl with the feel of that blade coming to bed itself in him. Cold steel . . .

Just the thought of it could turn a man loco.

Blood pounded into his brain and a wildness he had hoped never again to experience began to spill its red rage across Maffitt's thinking. He felt the head of this craziness and then, back of him, the breed snarled and there were sounds of a struggle.

Maffitt with a yell hurled himself at McQuirchee. McQuirchee's eyes sprang wide with shock as Maffitt crashed into him, impact carrying both men over the counter and the counter, with a rending of wood, over on top of them. McQuirchee screamed like a stuck pig when his head banged the floor. The counter was hampering Maffitt; it wasn't being much help to those gun slingers either but Maffitt, right then, was too busy to notice. He got a knee into McQuirchee's chest, hammering McQuirchee's head against the planks until the neck he had hold of had no more resistance than a rubber boot. Squirming free of the counter Maffitt slipped on the bloody floor.

It was all that saved him. He came down hard and the fall or the sledging racket of guns cleared some of the madness out of his mind; or maybe it was the crash-banging of slugs ripping through the wrecked counter and the miscellany of goods shelved back of him that finally brought him out of his terror.

He found himself sprawled against the slackness of McQuirchee — he almost puked staring into that dead face. He had some pretty bad moments before he recovered sufficiently to move again. With shaking hand he reached for the gun — that Army Remington Katherin had loaned him. All he found was empty leather.

He tried to push himself into the cracks of the floor as an upswing of panic got hold of him again. With sweat breaking through every pore of his body he fought the glaze from his eyes. He shuddered, his cold guts ready to crawl, when his prowling stare again touched McQuirchee. He felt around for the Remington, clammy as a polecat. Then he saw the glint of it, but it was too far away to reach without showing himself.

In half realized fragments many things came back to him, torn out of time and sequence, like that run-in he'd had with Ben Thompson at Dodge, that jamboree at the OK Corral when at Tombstone he had made common cause with the Clantons. Captain Bless got into his whirling thoughts — the way the man's glance had studied him. All the days of his past were filled with things left unfinished, all the hours of his nightmares lived with memories.

Suddenly he was conscious of the still-ness. He didn't think anyone had fallen asleep. McQuirchee's hardcases were waiting for him to give them something to shoot at.

They could afford to wait, damn them!

He glared around, eyes hunting some-thing he might use to defend himself. His glance tacked into McQuirchee and it came over him in a kind of dim dread how far he had gone along the road of no return. In the beginning he had never stopped to wonder about anything. He'd had a rein on his temper, on the alarms that triggered this wild streak, but somewhere he had lost it. A man could get that way in tight corners, as prone to panic as a spooky bronc. It was a sign and it bothered him.

Crouched there, listening, glance still trying to find some way out of this, he won-dered what the hell had become of that girl.

The quiet was like an ache. He shoved a hand across his cheeks, irascible pushing at the sweat, and the sound — at least to Maffitt — was harsh as boots slogging through gravel. He shrank down against the boards in expectation of a bullet. But nothing came. The stillness squeezed against his guts. It became a kind of drum beat by the pounding of his heart. *Trying to make him think he was alone in the place!*

He could picture the three of them squatted behind their guns, breathing through their teeth like a bunch of goddam fishes! He had his jaws apart, too. He closed his mouth disgustedly. McQuirchee had a gun. The crazy fool was laying on it!

It was nagging thoughts of the girl that put him in mind of the breed again. Fellow had probably slugged her. He was probably out there someplace with that knife in his teeth, trying to wriggle his way into this box through the back.

This became so unbearably real in Maffitt's mind his nerves wouldn't let him hold still any longer, even overriding his natural reluctance toward anything at all which might show them where he was. He needed that weapon and, knowing he couldn't get it until he got McQuirchee off it, he pushed the son of a bitch over. Five shots ripped through the wrecked counter practically in unison, three of the slugs driving into the trader like the slog of a cleaver going into cold meat. The others went into the rumple of blankets.

Maffitt hated the sight of that bright sticky blood. His stomach churned biliously but he had the gun now. He came onto his feet like a bull scrambling up and got off three shots before McQuirchee's jaspers could shake loose of their dumbfoundment. The nearest with squeezed-shut eyes doubled over, both hands convulsively shoved against his guts. A second skidded sideways with a leg knocked out from under him. The third, springing up with a yell, went straight through the window taking sash and all. The uproar was awful.

Maffitt, vaulting the wrecked counter, ran onto the porch. He saw the fellow, really heating his axles. Maffitt emptied McQuirchee's pistol. The departing man stumbled but did not go down. He didn't stop to pick any daisies, either. Still yelling he headed straight into the desert.

McQuirchee's gun, like the one Maffitt had lost back at Naco, was a Colt's .44 taking the rimfire cartridges he used in the Winchester he'd left on Afligido. He guessed he'd earn that three thousand if he ever got back with Afligido to claim it.

He reloaded from his belt and, swinging around, discovered Katherin. She was over by the saddle shed, appearing still to be more or less in one piece. She was trying to do something to the shoulder of her dress. If anyone else was around they were being mighty careful to stay out of sight.

"Where's that breed?" Maffitt called.

"He got away from me."

Maffitt said, "You able to move?"

"No bones broken, I guess, but I am hungry enough to eat dog stew." She started toward him, hitching her dress around.

Maffitt reckoned he could do with a little himself; the fight had used up all the good from those sandwiches. He took a squint at the sun. He wanted to get out of here but he knew they would be fools to ride away with empty bellies. "See if you can scrape something up —"

"I found your horse." She gave it like bad news, then said, "That brainless oaf took off on mine!"

"He didn't look like no conno soor," Maffitt grunted.

She eyed him blankly then managed a shaky laugh. "He wanted the black but Afligido couldn't see it." She lifted the pistol she'd once pointed at Maffitt. "I got off one round. He didn't wait for the other."

Maffitt hadn't known she even had the gun with her — must have had it cached down inside her dress someplace. He saw the torn shoulder she'd fastened together with a couple of thorns. He considered her guardedly and guessed by the lift of color her thoughts were traveling more or less in the same direction. "Well," he said gruffly, "there's no lack of horses." He scowled at the three McQuirchee's crew had left tied outside the middle pen. "That grulla ought to do. For a while, anyhow."

He slanched another look at her then said, turning away, "Sing out when you get that chuck dished up," and went back into the store.

The man he had shot through the stomach was dead. The other one, groaning, looked like the hinges of hell. All the fight was knocked out of him but the hate burning out of his mean little eyes was hot enough to fry eggs. Sensible thing would be to kill the guy now.

He picked up the fellow's pistol and pitched it back of the counter. He walked around, eyeing the shelves. He was mightily tempted to outfit them properly but a pack horse, he reckoned, would slow them down that much more and nothing would be gained if they had to turn loose of it. He did pick up and shake out a couple of blankets; these they would need when they got up into the mountains.

Left to himself he'd have been gone from here now. He found a pair of saddlebags and half filled them with .44-40s, threw in a few tins of tomatoes and peaches. He also filled the loops of his belt, deciding this was all the excess weight he could afford.

He went over then and examined the man's leg. It was a nasty-looking hole but the bones were all right. He found some sacking and bound it up and helped the fellow get into his pants again. "You better start hunting a sawbones," he said, looking into the snarling eyes.

The man didn't answer. Maffitt helped him up, watched him stagger outside. "Don't take that grulla," he called after him. He knew damned well he ought to settle this now; they wouldn't have had any scruples about killing.

But he just wasn't up to it. He remembered Burt Alvord telling him one time when Burt had been marshal of Willcox: "You better git shed of that soft streak, kid. They's just two kinds when it comes to people — live ones and goners. Never drag a gun without you aim to use it. Never set one off without you figger to kill."

6

He stood there, hand stretched out against
the wall — braced, really — trying to make
up his mind to a number of things, and all the
time he kept shaking and shuddering like all
the damned nerves in his body had come
loose. He couldn't even put good heart into
his cussing. He kept seeing those goddam
dying faces, and suddenly he threw up what
little was in him and hung there, racked and
soaking in his sweat.

Presently, furtively, he glared around
shamefaced and dragged the back of a hand
across his bitter mouth and, still twitching,
wiped the hand against the seat of his pants.
After what seemed a vast while of just
standing there he halfway got himself together and heard Katherin call. He shivered,
cold now and empty, feeling tired and
beaten. He thought of Cecil Breeding, snug
and comfortable at Bridle Bit, and Casas
filled with fury tearing the grass roots up

somewhere back of them; and he saw a bed in his mind and himself in it with Katherin and he was filled with disgust. He wished to hell he'd never climbed onto that damned balcony.

He got the saddlebags over a shoulder, grabbed up the blankets and quit the store. Leaving the porch he came into the full glare of the sun and stopped with a brassy taste of nausea to scowl back into the shambles.

"Hell with them!" he snarled, and tramped over to where the tied geldings stood pawing and whickering. He hung the bags over the corral's top pole, stacking the folded blankets on them.

The girl poked her head out of an oblong box that was obviously a cook shack. "Ready," she said again. With no sign of having heard, Maffitt, pulling off his stinking shirt, went over to the horse trough and sluiced himself off as well as he was able. He scrubbed his hands with sand and scrubbed the shirt with sand too, and sloshed it around and wrung it out and draped it across the poles to dry. He scowled at his hands and washed them again and stood for some moments looking hard toward the border through the slots of his eyes. He particularly studied several sun-struck patches where there may have been a suggestion of lifted dust.

He finally went on, coming into the shack where Katherin stood waiting, dropping onto a bench before the plate she had filled. "You go ahead," she said, "I've already had mine. I'll step out and keep watch."

He let her go. There'd been something in her tone or in the swirl of her eyes he couldn't quite fathom. He wolfed the food, neither knowing nor caring what it was, hardly tasting it. He drank the black coffee she'd poured into the tin cup and got up and refilled it from the battered blue pot. When his plate was clean he drank the dregs of the java directly from the pot, trying to wash some of the bad taste out of his head.

When he stepped out she had Afligido on the reins over by the trough. It seemed to him she deliberately avoided his eyes, appearing to be taken up with studying the backtrail. He leveled a scrinched look in that direction himself, discovering no more than he'd observed with the first glance. Wind out there, a dun glimmer of dust but, so far as he could see, nothing hostile, nothing to justify the look on her cheeks. It was hot of course but . . . He shook the blankets out and rolled them, hitching them securely to the back of the grulla's saddle.

He fetched the horse to the trough, the girl stepping away with Afligido to give them room. The black laid his ears back, showed his teeth a little and blew through his nose, but the girl had hold of him. She certainly wasn't afraid.

Maffitt looked at her covertly but whatever had been on her mind there was nothing of it showing, her glance meeting his with a composed indifference. Well, maybe not that exactly, but at any rate without any obvious constraint.

Watching the gelding drink with one ear cocked in the direction of Afligido, Maffitt tried to sort out if what he had sensed had been fear, revulsion or merely a natural diffidence sprung out of McQuirchee's talk from the book. He wasn't even sure there'd been anything. A man sour and touchy as he'd been right then could latch onto all manner of damn fool notions.

She said, "I can't believe they've any more than hardly got started. They surely aren't more than halfway . . ."

Maffitt's mouth stayed shut but his eyes said he wasn't banking on anything. He was obviously in a sweat to be gone. He got into his shirt, shoving the tails into his pants — the shirt was practically dry. He got the saddlebags then, tugged the slack from the cinches and came around to give Katherin a hand up. She managed a pale smile but got aboard the nervous gelding without touching Maffitt.

His cheeks turned leaner but he didn't say anything. He picked up the saddlebags and got onto Afligido, sharply reining the black around. "Lead off," he said. "I want to get to that creek by the shortest route."

By the sun it was close onto ten before they sighted it. They hadn't spoke a dozen words. If she felt like he did she was in no mood for idle conversation. "Turn up it," he said, "and stay in the water." Before following her he deliberately left sign indicating their direction. She noticed this and regarded him curiously.

"What they see here don't make no never mind. Maybe Casas will waste a little time prowling around. It's when we get out that we've got to be careful."

He kept crowding her, scowling, in a lather of impatience. Once Afligido nipped the grulla's rump. Twice he snapped off hanks of the gelding's tail hair. Maffit said nothing, one way or the other. Three times they passed ledgerock that would have taken them out without leaving much sign but each time she looked back Maffitt grimly shook his head.

They rode the creek's convolutions for the roughest part of two hours, ducking limbs, clawed by brush, harried by insects until the girl looked just about fit to be tied. Abruptly stopping her horse she skreaked around in the saddle. Sweat had plastered a strand of pulled-loose hair to her cheek. Red faced and furious she declared, "I'm getting out!"

"So long," Maffitt said.

Her eyes, widening, rounded, became nearly black. A single spot of color clung high up in either cheek. "Move," Maffitt said, "or get out of the way."

What her eyes showed then anyone could have read. Maffitt reckoned it was lucky he wasn't a white oak post or he'd have gone up in smoke. She slammed around and clouted the grulla with the whistling ends of her reins.

"Take it easy," Maffitt growled. "Be a long walk ahead if that geldin' breaks a leg."

No more droop of tired shoulders, he noticed. Her back looked stiff as a gunbarrel. Maffitt loosed a sour grin. If he felt any compassion for her bare scratched legs or for the ruin of her dress he concealed it admirably.

Twenty minutes later they came to another slant of negotiable ledge. It came out of the right bank and Maffitt said, "Haul up." He thought for a minute in her anger she was going to ignore him. Splashing across the shallow shelf he put Afligido up with her. He would have reached for the gelding's cheek strap had she not stopped before he could do so.

They glared at each other like cats on a back fence. She jerked her knee away from his. Maffitt said with a hard suffering patience, "We're leaving the creek —"

"Sure you're not doing this just for me?"

"Anyone," Maffitt said, "would know we was married."

Color whipped into her livid cheeks. "It's not a condition you'll need put up with for long!"

Maffitt looked at her. "Get down and lead your horse. I don't aim to leave any more sign than we have to. When the rock gives out get back in the saddle."

Her lips curled. "Yes, master." But she got down.

"Let your horse drink if he wants to," Maffitt said.

The grulla just stood there, indifferently, waiting. Katherin's eyes jeered at Maffitt. "You can walk a horse half a day through water but even you can't make him drink. Too bad he's not a woman." She hauled the gelding up onto the ledge, let him shake while she wrung some of the water out of her skirts — there'd been lace on the under one but there wasn't any now.

Maffitt swung down and led the black stallion out, searching the easiest going to avoid all he could leaving marks on the rock. He emptied the water out of his boots and tugged them back on and, scanning the eastern view, at last, said, "Head for them sand hills."

She looked around with curled lip. "That's not the quickest way to El Paso."

He stared. "I'm not going to El Paso."

Her eyes widened. She bit her lip. "You want to find yourself back in Mexico?"

"That'll be just fine."

"You won't think it's fine if we get picked up by Rurales!"

When he didn't rise to that she said, "Suppose we bump into Casas? If his thinking goes the way you figured and he turns downstream —"

"He won't be downstream by the time we get over there." He scowled at her bare feet; she'd lost both slippers in the water and been too bull-headed to pick them up. "Quit jawin' and get moving."

Her chin swept up. She flounced about and struck out.

She was a sight, he thought. He gave a

grudging admiration — in his head where it wouldn't hurt her. He picked up Afligido's reins and tramped after her. The ledge was an outcrop. In fifty yards they were off it, swinging up into leather for the trip to the sand which he judged to be possibly three miles away. The ground was wind crusted adobe, flat and hot, grown sparsely to greasewood and completely open from the rocks above the creek. They couldn't afford to run the horses. He could only hope Casas' outfit, or anyone else on their trail, wouldn't reach this point before they got into the hills.

It didn't seem too likely. They'd come a good many miles from Naco. But if Casas or her father were sufficiently riled — even so, he didn't see how they could reach this place before the girl and himself could get behind some of those hills. There was nothing back in the direction they'd come but badlands, rock and lava crisscrossed with gullies and box canyons. Of course if the pursuit had thought to fetch along extra horses . . . Or if Casas or the sheriff had reason to anticipate the true direction of their flight . . .

Barr, anyway, would probably use the telegraph. This was Maffitt's principle reason for pointing the way he was right now. There'd be no poles in this stretch of country. And no sheriffs in Mexico to take up the chase or put out to waylay them. Just let him, by God, set foot in Sonora and her old man could whistle!

Sonora wouldn't be any help against Casas but he'd played tag with Casas before and got away from him. The law wasn't a thing a man could easily elude and its long arm was a blackening shadow in his thoughts — all too vividly he could imagine its fingers spreading to catch and haul him back — its rewards and its bounty hunters. He'd done a few things he wasn't real proud of but he hadn't ever before given the law cause to hunt him, and the thought of it now was like a sword hanging over him.

The girl's bright notion of blocking her father by marriage and the witnesses they were to have left at McQuirchee's had blown up in their faces. They'd be remembered all right, but any witnesses left were going to be hog wild to hang him, particularly that guy with the hole in his leg. He wouldn't be talking about no marrying!

He was stuck with the girl now tighter than ever — she was his out if the law got its hands on him, the only one who could give him a clean slate. Not that he had much confidence she would do so; it was simply a case of having no other defense.

His thoughts were like horses hitched to a treadmill. Around and around in a hopeless circle. And every mile of this flight was taking him farther from Bridle Bit and Breeding. He was stuffed to the gills with frustration and fury, hotter than a five-dollar pistol.

The only ray of light in the whole damned business was the single probability that Casas and Sheriff Barr would not be teaming up on this deal. Casas wanted the horse but would be extremely reluctant to share his troubles with the law; if they had aimed to do that they could have stopped him south of the border. They could have stopped him at Naco. The law's current interest — as personified by Barr — could work to Casas' disadvantage.

This didn't cheer Maffitt much. Every man's hand was against him. Try as you might you couldn't get around that.

They got into the sand hills, still apparently unsighted. At least Maffitt saw no evidence of pursuit. He kept the pace to an easy walk. A man could be frightened without losing his head. It had seemed these last couple of miles he could not be in much worse of a jackpot, but deep inside he knew better than that. It would be worse to be dead, and they could damned soon be if anything happened to these horses out here.

A half hour later they came out of the sand, faced with rolling grasslands yellow from drought that climbed in a long gradual lift toward mountains hanging blue in the distance. Now if only a wind would spring up back there they wouldn't have to worry about any tracks they had left. Even the shape of those hills could be changed by a good wind. But Maffitt couldn't recall ever having heard of a good one, nor could he find any sign of one about to spring up. Like the rains, wind seldom came when a man most direly . . .

Katherin said, looking back, "Do you have any idea where we are?"

"I'd a heap sooner know where our friends are right now."

"You must have something in mind," she said, waiting for him. "No one would be fool enough —"

"A man would have to be pretty damn foolish to get stuck with the sort of deal I'm fixed up with."

Her cheeks showed the shot had got home. Her eyes held an open resentment and then, surprisingly, became contrite. "I don't suppose you have much reason to think very highly of me. You don't know the spot I was in — you're not a woman. You can't imagine what it's like to be dependent for everything. For your clothes, shelter, the very food that goes into you. A woman, by the very nature of her complexities, values security . . ."

"Kind of late," Maffitt said, "to be thinking about that."

Her chin came up, stubborn. "I've thought about it — plenty. But care — even kindness — can become an intolerable burden. I don't expect you to understand. A man," she said, keeping a wary interval between them, "looking at a woman takes note of only what he sees. If she's reasonably easy to look at, has social grace, attractive clothes, carries herself with any kind of distinction, she becomes a fool in his mind to do the sort of thing I've done."

"If you can call sticking a man up at gun point —"

"I got you out of that, didn't I? You're not lying back there in some alley. You're not dead. You're not in jail."

Maffitt, a little cynically, recalled her words about kindness. But all he said was, "Who'd he want you to marry?"

She peered at him, startled.

He said, "It almost had to be some man. If there's anything will turn a woman plumb loco a man can generally be found at the bottom of it."

She looked at him carefully. "Dad wanted me to marry Casas."

7

If the sky had fallen Maffitt hardly could have been more thrown out of countenance. A kind of clamorous blackness closed about him through which he bitterly watched her face without seeing it. What he saw, graphic as the strokes in a tally book, was the Law and Chico Casas teamed up to run him down, the one thing he'd figured he was safe against.

He was too stirred up to swear. A paralysis had suddenly laid hold of him. He felt like a rat backed into a corner and the likeness pulled the lips off his teeth. He caught the stark look in her abruptly wide eyes, became aware that he had hold of her, the neck of her dress bunched together in his grip, had her yanked half out of the saddle.

In some queer way the knowledge shocked him. Even in the greater shock of what she had just told him this knowledge shook him. He had no remembrance of reaching for her. It frightened him, twisting that all-gone coldness in his middle with the same half strangling sickness he'd felt when he found McQuirchee dead.

He had a curious impression it was somebody else standing back in his mind seeing all this, watching the fury churning through that damned fool. His knees shook against the sweating sides of his horse. Yet he was still of two minds when he reluctantly let go of her, settling back into leather with an almost audible snarl.

He watched color come through the blanched quiver of her cheeks, saw her throat constrict, the jerky lift and falling of her breasts as she took air. The pink tip of her tongue crept across the red lips and some remote part of him took cognizance of their curves. She seemed to have trouble getting words to move over them. They finally came with a little rush of sound, tumbling over each other as, voice found, she cried defensively, "If I'd told you sooner —"

A down-chopping swing of his hand cut her off. He put the black into motion. He could control these things but not his thoughts. She had called the turn. If she'd told him back there at Naco he would never have been sucked into this, gun or no gun! It was too late now — too late even to get back to that creek. They were damned near into Mexico.

He slanched a bleak look at the mountains. They showed visibly nearer, not close but near enough to reveal other colors than that predominating blue; maybe thirty miles away. Maybe closer. He didn't know anything about them, but they were Mexican mountains and still his best bet. They'd have plenty of places where a man could hide and this was his strongest urge right now, to crawl into some hole and drag it in after him — after *them*. He was still stuck with her.

The black was sidling around, blowing and shaking like an Apache rattling a sackful of bones; and Maffitt, recollecting how sensitive some horses were to the moods of their riders, took hold of Afligido with the renewed grip of his legs.

The girl's horse suddenly went into the air, snapping, squealing with both ears back. Before Maffitt could grab the crazed horse had whirled, unseating the girl, coming down on bunched hoofs like a slide letting go. Maffitt heard the buzz then, saw the tail of the snake — green and yellow, a big tiger rattler, the kind the Hopis used in their rituals. The grulla stomped it, stood shaking, nostrils distended, left front leg commencing to swell.

The girl picked herself up as Maffitt swung down, keeping hold of the black's reins, dragging him nearer as he bent to make sure the gelding had been struck. It had. Twice.

Maffitt, cursing in frustration, glowered as though the horse had got itself bit deliberately.

"I'm sorry," Katherin said, working the rag of the blue dress down over her legs as if modesty were something she'd be able to ride. "I should have been watching . . ." She reached for the reins.

Maffitt struck her hand away. "Keep back. You never know what a snake-bit bronc will do. You'll have to ride Afligido." He saw the self blame in her eyes, knew she was miserable. She wanted to be friends now, was holding out the purse from which she'd paid McQuirchee. "Would you take care of this for me?"

"Climb aboard," Maffitt growled, clamping one hand in the stallion's ragged mane, holding onto the reins and cheek strap with the other.

Her eyes searched his dark face unfathomably, seeing him now as he so seldom appeared, driven and harried, prey to the same fears that gnawed other men; thinking, she knew, of all the odds stacked against him, grown immeasurably more disheartening in these few moments. Sweat was an oily shine through the whiskers sticking out of his cheeks like black wires. His guard was down and no confidence came out of him, only his fury and this wicked impatience.

She caught hold of the stirrup, twisting it toward the thrust of bare toes. She couldn't help showing a good deal of leg as she went up but Maffitt never looked at her. "Easy boy — easy," he cautioned as the stallion, unused to skirts touching him as he was to the girl, stiffened with skin tight, starting to tremble. Maffitt let go of the mane to run a hand soothingly over taut muscles in the way of one thoroughly familiar with horses.

Katherin felt the black's fright and some of it got into her. Maffitt kept talking to the horse. Now, taking hold of a twist of her skirt, he brought it forward for the stallion to sniff at, then he eased one foot forward. The girl felt the outblown wash of his breath, the bristly stubble of nudging lips. She let him nuzzle the foot. His ears came up. He blew again, gradually quieting. She knew then he had accepted her.

Maffitt, handing her the reins, let go of the cheek strap, moving back to the grulla. He stared for some while before he dragged off the saddle, reluctantly abandoning it. And the blankets. He studied the gelding's leg again, keeping well out of the reach of broad teeth. Straightening he pulled off the bridle, leaving it, too.

He came back to the stallion. Removing the saddlebags he threw out the tinned stuff, stuffed a handful of cartridges into each of his front pockets and dropped the bags with the rest he was discarding.

"You can't —"

His eyes whipped around at her. "Lead out!" he said, tone brooking no argument. She flushed, shortening the reins; but, womanlike, had to find something to put voice to. "Surely you're not going to leave that poor horse . . ."

"I'm not going to fire no gun at him!" he snarled. He got the canteen and rifle off the abandoned saddle. He scowled dubiously at the rope but finally salvaged it, tying it securely to the saddle under the girl. "Sometimes they'll pull through. Get moving."

She eased the black into motion.

"Give him more rein."

Her back stiffened rebelliously but she slacked up some. Afligido stepped out and Maffitt came up alongside of him, ready to reach if the big horse showed any sign of wanting to bolt.

The snake-bit grulla nickered piteously.

When no one stopped or looked back he pawed the ground with his good foot. Shaking nervously, he set out after them.

The sun boiled down. Maffitt's shirt turned dark and stuck in great patches. He scrinched a glance back, scowling, to peer at their shadows. He stared ahead, grimly bitter, and finally dragged off his hat. "Better put this on," he said, reaching it up to her.

"I'm all right."

Maffitt, eyeing her, irascibly put the hat back on. The gun she had loaned him someway came up for notice and he cursed his carelessness in leaving it behind. He thought also of those two breed toddlers who'd disappeared after the shooting and the woman or women he hadn't even laid eyes on. Apaches, probably. They may have cleared out but not likely. They'd find the gun. When Barr came along it would be the first thing he'd look at. And that jasper who'd took out, hitting the high spots with the leaps of a rabbit — he'd be back shooting off his mouth.

You could count on that. Even if the girl's old man never showed, Casas would get there — was probably there now. He'd see the gun too and he would listen to anyone. Maffitt wished now he'd taken that money off McQuirchee, or the purse Katherin had offered. He had a faculty for getting squeamish over the wrong kind of things. It wasn't the fact of having killed that turned his stomach about McQuirchee — he'd come near enough before to see the black pit staring up at him. What unsettled him — like with the girl — was the evidence of how far he would go in the red fog of temper without even realizing what he was doing. He was two different people. It scared the hell out of him.

He shoved out a hand and caught hold of the stirrup, all mixed up in his head — disturbed even further when his hand brushed the girl's foot. She lifted it, thinking he was going to swing up.

He took back the hand, growling, rasping his cheeks with it. She understood then how badly he was worried, that he'd been minded to push Afligido a little. Covertly watching she saw him get hold of himself, jaws clamped again, gone into a black study, probably examining their prospects, brooding over the things he'd got to do and probably couldn't. She shivered a little, hot as she was.

The sun had passed its peak, was on its westward ride now. Their shadows moved awry and foreshortened, bobbing about an arm's length ahead across tawny ground that was giving away now to widening stretches of sand as the lemon grass petered out into brittle clumps.

Maffitt was counting on that creek slowing Casas. He could still see a chance, almighty slim but worth clawing for, if he could keep his feet under him and hang onto this horse.

He looked back and discovered the grulla still following. The gelding's head was down and that left leg from forearm to fetlock looked puffed as a teased toad. He was still coming, poor devil, but he was half a mile back and, although the thought was tinged with guilt, Maffitt was glad he had done the sensible thing. There was no dust showing and he was glad of that, too, though he reckoned Casas' bunch to be back of those hills and there was no hiding now this side of the mountains.

He pulled the chin off his shoulder. They didn't look to have gotten any noticeably nearer.

High-heeled boots. Maffitt cursed the tight fit of them. His feet felt on fire. The sand clutched at them, hampering him, and his throat was like cotton in this stifling glare. He still had the canteen off the abandoned saddle but wouldn't let himself touch it. The rifle he was toting grew heavier with every step.

Maffitt had been hoping to get under cover before the Mexican got to where he could see them. He couldn't count on this now. Losing the grulla had played hell with everything. At best they were likely fifteen miles from the nearest slope. Couldn't hide their tracks anyway but it might have helped if Casas had to hunt for them as he would have had if they'd got into the maze of gullies and washes that just about had to be somewhere ahead of them. Once Casas sighted them he'd be likely to make a race of it. Not even Afligido, big and powerful as he was, could put up much of a show carrying double.

Damn the heat! He couldn't see how the girl stood it, bareheaded and not used to what she'd been through since Naco. Her face was the color of cooked lobster. Her hair was a snarled tangle of loose ends like a mare's nest. Her shoulders drooped with fatigue, her bloodshot eyes were almost shut yet never a word of complaint had come out of her.

Hell's holey halfboots! Maffitt snarled, catching up with himself. Only a goddam idiot would be caught feeling sorry for the cause of all his troubles! She was doing what she wanted — she was having her way. If she'd kept her wits about her she'd be riding the grulla and they would still have a fair-to-middling chance of getting clear. He growled, glanced again quartering over the dun distances ahead of them. He hated looking back, but gnawing anxieties finally got the best of him.

No dust yet. But the grulla was now a long mile behind them.

Maffitt scowled at the girl. He had to try twice before he could work up enough spit to talk with. Even then what he heard had the sound of a rusted gate hinge. "Let's have the rest of it."

She didn't look around but she heard him all right; he could tell by the way her lips tightened up. She said finally, "You've got it all."

"Not quite. Most fellers I know would skin their daughters alive if they so much as twisted a look at a chili. What's Casas got on him?"

She seemed to square herself up to it. "Dad's not bad, only weak. He never has had much of a knack for making money. The big breaks always seem to pass him by. He never speaks of Mother — she ran off with a salesman. She —"

"Let's get back to your old man."

Her eyes stayed in front of her. "He's a lot like you —"

"I'm not weak," Maffitt growled, and glared at her, affronted.

"He got broody," Katherin said. "He went badly in debt trying to keep up appearances. I suspect he felt put upon yet he was determined to send me away to an expensive school in the East — I hated every minute of it." She considered him a moment, brushing the hair back off her cheek. "I can't stand being cramped . . ." Her glance dropped back to a point between the stallion's ears. "I guess he couldn't, either. He was never cut out to be in business, I was still pretty young when he got a badge pinned on him. It didn't bring in much money —"

"Get to Casas."

Her eyes came around at him, hard and bright. "You've got to understand how he got into this mess —"

"I know how he got into it. Little things! Give an inch here, give a couple more there. Some people just can't do enough for —"

"He always said things were going to be different when he got to be sheriff . . ."

"But it was the same old sevens and eights," Maffitt said, "only now they wore boots and there was nails pounded into them."

She said thoughtfully, "Yes. The old sheriff got sick and Dad stepped into the job. He sent me off to become a lady —"

"And when you got back he was hobnobbin' with Casas."

"Not exactly. They were in some kind of business together."

"Sure," Maffitt nodded. "Man with a badge can get in plenty of business." His tone held the bitterness of remembrance. "Hard to let go and harder still to turn loose of. But," he smiled wryly, "a man's never a crook until he's caught, so Casas had him. They can see the mistakes of others — bein' quick with hindsight and judgments, each in his own head figuring himself a cut or two above fallin' into such potholes. Sometimes they are. An occasional few."

"I suppose," she said, "you're one of the smart ones."

Maffitt didn't answer, it having suddenly occurred to him that first he'd better pick the horse out of his own eye. All the time he'd been holding the law up to scorn, plodding along beside the big black, a considerable segment of their immediate environment had been concealed from his attention by the proximity of the horse.

Dropping back now to look beyond Afligido, hatbrim low and eyes scrinched against the glare, he was relieved to discover no pillar of dust. This relief was of short duration. He was perturbed to make out in the following moment the dark dot of a horseman coming up from the south.

The girl, stopping the black, searched his sun-blackened cheeks with a quickening alarm. "What is it?"

Maffitt waved her on with a bleak impatience. He'd have given something right then to have had a glass to put on that hombre. He couldn't even be sure the man had any interest in them, but he knew how to find out. Making sure, first of all, that there was still no sign in the west of Casas, he crossed around to the right and caught hold of the stirrup. "Lift him into a lope."

Katherin tightened her knees. The big black plunged forward. The tiny shape of the horsebacker in the south altered course; and now there was dust — enough to indicate the man's plain intention. The girl saw this, too. "You think he means to intercept us?"

"Pull him down," Maffitt panted. Letting go of the oxbow he dropped back to peer west again into the bare regions they had so recently traversed. He took enough time to break through the heat distortions and sundance before he dared accept the total lack his eyes declared. Even the grulla was still, standing head down and unmoving the best part of two miles behind them in the center, it appeared, of a shimmering lake that had no existence.

Now Maffitt's glance, hard as stone, swept north, scouring the country with a terrible intensity. So far as he could tell there was nobody north of him but he couldn't accept this; he could only be sure that there was nobody showing. Somewhere, west, behind those sand hills, Casas and his outfit would be hard on their trail. There might be others in the north.

His stare, swinging front again as he broke into a stumbling run, picked up the mountains, and all his experience placed them still the best bet — if he could reach them. He overtook the girl and the horse and, breathing hard, reclaimed the stirrup. In the south the solitary rider, nearer now and plainer, had eased his mount into the walk he'd abandoned, confident beyond all likelihood that well ahead of dark he'd come up with Maffitt. Maffitt thought so too and, reaching down, loosened McQuirchee's gun in the holster at his thigh.

No matter what reserves Afligido might call on he was still a tired horse with near a hundred miles behind him. They might be two hours from Mexico or crossing the border right now. Neither the one nor the other would mean anything to Casas. Or to that fellow off yonder. He was going to come into their way whether school kept or not.

The inevitability of this certainty was maddening to Maffitt. The only alternative to crossing trails with the fellow was to swing north at once. Their only real hope, as Maffitt saw it, lay in reaching and getting into those mountains which were surely Mexican and, by the same token, presumably without communications. If they were going to have to walk over this ranny to make it then Maffitt was prepared to walk over the son of a bitch.

Riding into the north held no assurance of safety and Maffitt, though he frequently denied it, was as bound by convention as the next, as obligated in his way to keep up appearances as Katherin's starpacking father. To run away from this galoot so plainly set on coming up with them was to admit a culpability Maffitt couldn't stomach.

He didn't see how the fellow could have any connection with Barr or Casas. He'd come out of the south — maybe out of the southwest — but unless he'd had more changes of horses than seemed reasonable he could hardly have come from Naco since the girl and Maffitt had quit the place.

Time was a pacer circling the treadmill of Maffitt's recurrent hopes and fears. The glare and the brassy rays of the sun became almost more than a man could put up with. The whole country shimmered and writhed in heat. Their shadows grew longer, grotesquely lurching ahead as though, jibing and sneering, they would run off and leave them. Maffitt clamped his jaws against the frightening urge to push Afligido.

He covertly studied the girl. More damn guts than you could hang on a fencepost! She was a piece, all right. He could feel the wild pull of her flesh calling his flesh, the woman hunger stirring deep in his loins like an awakening giant. Married him, hadn't she? Be hard to claim she'd had her eyes shut.

Queer how danger always sharpened a man's appetites. She was his — woman. No matter how come, his to do with whatever he wanted. She'd said in name only but she was too smart to really think that. She was old enough to know, by God, no man with any right to a woman . . .

He yanked his thoughts back away from such vistas. Plenty of time for that in the mountains; waiting a little never hurt anyone. Postponement only made realization sweeter.

Stamping clear of these notions Maffitt suddenly cursed. That carbine packer had got a whole heap nearer — no doubt now what they were going to be up against. Maffitt couldn't yet make out the fellow's looks but he could see well enough what the damned Paul Pry was wearing! Maffitt reached out, halfway snarling, clamping a fist hard about the black's reins.

They might still make a run for it. But not for long, mounted double. And when they were caught guilt would be established by evidence of flight.

Maffitt, glowering, set out for the man, hauling the black horse after him.

8

The girl had seen the garb too but her eyes weren't as sharp in this glare as necessity plus experience had managed to hone Maffitt's. She said nervously, "That's a uniform, isn't it? Border Patrol?"

Maffitt had no patience with foolish questions. The fellow had noted their changed course and swung his own mount. He came up with authority but not foolhardily, slanching in on Maffitt's right, carbine tipped across his crotch with no attempt at any semblance of casualness.

His eyes were a frosty blue and plainly used to dealing with prevaricators. He flushed a little when his glance went over Katherin's legs but he didn't touch his hat or deflect the readiness of his weapon by the slightest degree. "You took long enough coming around," he said curtly.

Maffitt scowled. "You see any telescopes screwed to my eyes? I got a woman to think about! Way it looked, by God, no man in his right mind would of got within a mile of you!"

Those appraising eyes while continuing to watch Maffitt managed, Maffitt noticed, to take in everything about them. Inscrutability covered this fellow thick as the dust that grayly draped every inch of him. He was no rookie nor minded to be taken for one.

"I'm listening," he said.

Maffitt's eyes skewered around like a dog's hunting cover. It had never once come into his head they might find themselves confronted with the patrol. He knew how this looked. He resorted to bluster.

The man with the carbine cut him off before he'd got even well into the start of it. "That doesn't explain your aiming for those mountains. Any reason you couldn't have gone by a port of entry?"

"Jesus Christ, man! You expect me to go forty miles out of my way just to satisfy a bunch of —"

"No need to get your back up. Let's have a look at your papers."

Maffitt, swallowing audibly, looked like a man who had just gone home to find his whole family scalped. "Papers . . ."

"You've a permit for crossing the border haven't you?"

Maffitt shifted his weight from one boot to the other. He let go of the black's reins. The girl cut in quickly, "I'm Katherin Maffitt. Dale, there, is my husband — we just got married this morning." She saw the officer's glance pass over the bedraggled dress. Fetching up a pale smile she held out the folded marriage certificate. The trooper gave it no attention at all. Ignoring the blackness of Maffitt's stare she said, plowing on, "It's been pretty hectic . . . We've been in the saddle —"

"Couldn't your husband manage to find you a horse, or is it him that hasn't got one?"

"A snake bit mine. The reason we've been trying to get into those mountains is my father — Sheriff Barr of Cochise County —" she paused a moment, embarrassed, "has never really cared much for Dale. We're afraid he's sent warnings to all ports of entry. We ran away to get married. He's probably after us right now."

No man could doubt she was telling the truth. Some of the stiffness went out of Maffitt's look when the obvious stirrings of sympathy began to thaw the man's mouth a little. The carbine toter's opinion plainly followed the expressed bent of her father's so far as Maffitt was concerned but taking the extended certificate now the border man, even with half his glance, could see that it substantiated what she had told him.

Dourly regarding the wreck of her dress he handed it back. Her eyes, her talk and the paper had convinced him, but the big black still appeared to stick in his craw. "That's a Mexican brand on that horse," he said to Maffitt. "You got a bill of sale for him?"

Maffitt started to reach for it and bitterly recollected it was back at the post, torn up by McQuirchee. A dozen thoughts wildly raced through his head but none of the things he might have said would come out of him. Be a waste of breath. The truth was useless: to admit he'd shot anyone could turn out to be as bad as being taken for a horse thief. He dragged out the receipt showing the duty he'd paid Bless back in Naco. "I don't have it with me but maybe this'll do."

He might have made a little better impression if he had let the border man hoe his own parsnips but, in the way of most people caught in a wringer, Maffitt had to talk, had to point up the obvious. "I would hardly have got through Customs," he growled, "if there'd been any doubt about my right to the horse."

It rubbed the man the wrong way. Katherin, biting her lips, saw the hardening of his eyes. The muscles swelled along his jaws and he said in a cold thin quiet, "That's a pretty valuable animal. A feller figuring to take him out of the country would have to be uncommon stupid not to provide himself with the proper credentials. I'm not doubting the young lady's story — far as it goes — but I'll have to ask you to come into town with me. If this deal's on the level you can cross below Mimbres and jog right along to wherever you're bound for."

Meanwhile Cecil Breeding, back at Bridle Bit, a costly cigar gripped between his yellow teeth, was trying to find a little comfort in the shade of the verandah. Only now was he at last beginning to throw off the sense of panic instilled in him by Maffitt's recent and wholly unexpected visit. It wasn't that he had actually anything to fear — he had covered his tracks in the matter of Maffitt's father, in the matter too of this swindle by which he had become sole owner of one of the most profitable ranching operations in the south-central part of the Territory. But with a fellow like Maffitt a man never knew. While he never in this world would have been able to prove anything, he might have made Breeding's tenure extremely uncomfortable — not to say dangerous.

Any large ranch has its fringe of enemies, the incompetent, the envious, the have-nots in all their categories. There were plenty roundabout who would like nothing better than to see Breeding squirm. They stayed in line because the size and caliber of Bridle Bit's crew and resources kept them there, but had trouble developed they would have been at his throat like a pack of wolves.

Breeding had no delusions about himself. He was a grasper, avaricious, with no more scruples than a bull on the peck; behind these things he was an arrant coward. He had got to his high place by exploiting the weaknesses of others.

Old Man Maffitt had been a natural; a born stockman, bull-headed as they came. It had taken no great ingenuity on Breedings's part to drive the old fool to the brink of drink measures. He wanted his cake while he still had some teeth to put into it. He had locked the old man up in his room and poured whisky down him until hell wouldn't have it.

Vechel Harris, the Bridle Bit segundo, was the only hombre with any real inkling of what actually had happened and Vechel wasn't likely to run off at the mouth. He had too good a thing here. In addition to which Breeding, down in writing, had enough on

Vechel Harris to put the man away for the rest of his natural. Both of them knew it. And so in a kind of uneasy truce they made the most of their opportunities, presenting a united front to the world. By themselves as they were now, not having to keep up appearances, they could let down and say pretty much what they felt like.

Harris, sitting slouched over a drink, said apropos of nothing in their talk, "Looks like you handled that feller about right. If he'd been comin' back he ought to got here by now. For a thousand bucks you're rid of him cheap. He was a pretty tough biscuit."

Breeding looked at his foreman distastefully, resenting the overbearing assurance that most of the time he found profitable to cultivate. Harris was burly, more resembling a shaggy boar than a man, black all over, with muscles that strained every bind of his shirt, not tall but broad with skin like a rhino. A cropped and bristling mustache half concealed the arrogant curl of sneering lips. The man wasn't stupid like nine-tenths of the hardcases currently on the ranch payroll. He was cunning and sharp.

Breeding didn't care to have any discussion of Maffitt and, though he angrily suspected Harris was leading up to something, he couldn't steer his thoughts away from it.

Maffitt turning up after all this time had given him a bad jolt and the ripples that had spread from it were still running through his head.

Harris grinned. "Relax. You've seen the last of him. They'd never let that black out of hand for no thousand. They've cleaned up more'n that in one race. So what would he do? Try to steal him, like you figured. There's one thing you got to hand to them Mexes. When they've reason to get shed of a guy they get shed of him."

Breeding wanted to believe it but he was still filled with doubts. "Hell," Harris said, "say he gets away with it. The guy knows horses. He ain't comin' back with that black for two thousand! So what's eatin' you? Either way you win. If Olivares settles his hash, okay. If he don't the guy's a horse thief twice over. You made a deal with him to buy you that horse, you put dough in his mitt. If he makes off with the stud you got nothin' to worry about. Any time he turns up — if he's that big a yap — you can drop the jail on 'im."

Like Katherin's admissions to the man with the carbine this was all very well so far as it went. But Breeding wanted the horse. It was a want he'd been nursing a considerable while. That black would round out what he

111

had very neatly. At stud it would fetch people of means from all over, advancing his repute as a breeder of fine saddlers, horses that could do, that could get up and go. As sire of his colts and fillies it had a very practical attraction. He had long ago decided he was going to have the horse; but of the two, right now, Maffitt's scalp was the more important.

When Harris presently left without having voiced whatever he'd been angling around toward, Breeding went in and sat down at his desk. He remained with a look of brooding, hunched over it unmoving while the shadows filled the corners of the room and the grandfather clock that had come by covered wagon over the windswept miles from the present Maffitt's mother's folks solemnly tick-tocked the run of minutes. Pulling paper toward him Breeding finally picked up his pen.

"My Dear General," he wrote. "Two weeks ago a man named Maffitt left here en route for your ranch with three thousand dollars (U.S. money) to negotiate ultimate purchase your good stallion Afligido. Disquieting rumors have since come to my attention suggesting the man may never have reached you . . ."

A wink, Breeding grinned, would be as

good as a nod to the fellow who was going to be reading this. Three thousand should be enough to spur even a governor and all it would cost was the thousand Breeding had already crossed off the books.

Afligido could wait.

9

Maffitt stood there dry-mouthed, widened eyes blankly focused on the blur of those dusty cheeks, only seeing in his mind all the things he'd been afraid of. And the red fog creeping round them.

The trooper's glance toughened noticeably. "I'll have to ask you for that pistol."

There was ice in Maffitt's belly. His head felt like it was in the grip of rawhide and he saw the swirls of red mist rising in the fruitlessness of all past care, in the irony of being caught up to his armpits in a mirage of illegalities for which his innocence was neither excuse nor help. *Give a dog a bad name . . .*

"There's been a big black pretty much like this one," the border man said, "mixed up with a bunch that's been running guns —"

"Oh, but —" Katherin began; and that was when Maffitt leaped. Off the ground like a cougar he was so swift, so savagely sure, the man had no chance to duck or bring up his carbine. The gun went off as it was knocked from his grasp, and he followed it over the back of his horse with Maffitt's grip round his throat and Maffitt's weight, as they struck, shaking out of him what little air he'd kept hold of.

The fellow had been taken by surprise, caught with attention divided, made to look a fool, but he was as desperate now as Maffitt — warned by Maffitt's ferocity. He wriggled and squirmed, thrashing out with his legs, hammering Maffitt with a fury of short blows; someway he managed to break Maffitt's hold.

He was up, purple-faced, gulping air like a windbroke bronc, when Maffitt slammed into him with a battery of lefts and rights. Staggering, wheezing, he kept backing away with his eyes like chips of glittering glass. Twice he tried to bring iron from leather but Maffitt gave him no time, forcing him to lift leaden arms, keeping him off balance, hammering him unmercifully. One of Maffitt's connecting swings spun him like a top, dropping him, wobbly, onto one knee, only braced arms keeping him clear of the ground.

Maffitt dived in and hit nothing but dirt, the man jerking away, clawing again at his holster as he came onto his feet. Maffitt rolled, twisting frantically to get at McQuirchee's gun.

Both men in their absorption had forgotten the girl. The trooper's pistol was clearing leather when her voice rang out sharply. "Stop it — both of you!"

She stood white-faced with the derringer covering them. The border man's look was intolerably angry; his glance, ignoring her two-barreled popgun, appearing strongly inclined to go on with it. Maffitt, never sparing her a shred of his attention, cleared McQuirchee's pistol and was bringing it up in single mindedness of purpose when the girl's weapon spoke, kicking sand in his face.

Maffitt's whipped-around stare was like a curse.

In those moments, so perilously fraught with all the ingredients of disaster, Katherin's eyes never wavered. It took rare courage to face that pair with a gun that couldn't have more than one shot left, seeing — as she must — the killing rage that was prodding both of them. "There's been enough blood," she said. "All we want is his horse."

She saw the trooper's cheeks whiten. He couldn't know her gun was empty. When he shrugged, letting go of his pistol, the relief of it almost undid her. Her glance picked up Maffitt barely in time. His lips were set in bitter lines; every hunched-up ridge of that frustrated face called her fool as he shoved McQuirchee's iron back in leather and got irascibly onto his feet.

Katherin said to the trooper, "Unbuckle your belt and step away from it."

The man's look was bleak. Dark with rage he obeyed the unwinking muzzle of her gun. "Get your canteen off the horse," she said, "and start hiking."

"Better kill him now," Maffitt growled. "Puttin' him afoot in this kind of country —"

"It's hardly twelve miles to Antelope Wells. He'll make it," she said, watching the man. He got the canteen and looked back at them with the kind of hard steadiness that said plainer than words he meant to know them again if he ever ran onto them. He hitched the strap over his shoulder and set off without comment, wallowing a little as his boots dug into the drifted sand.

Moving to the confiscated horse Maffitt caught up the reins and went into the saddle. Wheeling the horse around he put a hard look over the backtrail and slapped back his heels, lifting the animal into a lope. Katherin, boarding Afligido, saw the glint of the half-buried carbine and was about to get back down when Maffitt's voice curving out of a snarl yelled: "Leave it lay!"

She put the black after him. There was a hard, controlled impatience in Maffitt's handling of the new horse which presently caused her to look behind. Her widening glance saw the dust at once. The man they'd set afoot was a black dot some way this side of and a bit to the north of it. There was not a great deal and it was still a good stretch back of them but not too far for her to spot the bobbing dark smudge ahead of it that she knew were the shapes of mounted men.

She called out her discovery. Maffitt neither turned nor spoke. But he pulled down into a kind of loose rack, going on in this way for another couple miles before easing their pace back into a walk. Now he looked behind, studying, gauging, bleakly chalking up the probabilities.

But he held to the walk. They had, Katherin estimated, perhaps a ten-mile lead; there was approximately the same spread of distance between their current position and the folds of ground which seemingly made up the nearer footslopes of the mountains. If they could get into these with any kind of margin they would still have a pretty fair chance, but Maffitt wasn't ready to show their hand in open flight. And he was smart in that. Endurance was what counted. The horse between his legs showed bottom — outcrossed to some thoroughbred probably — but it certainly wasn't in Afligido's class. However it hadn't put behind it the miles Afligido had; so they were, for the moment, pretty well matched. They still had run in them but would go a lot farther if the run wasn't called for.

These were things Katherin, with her Western raising, understood. That hard impatience was still prodding Maffitt but he was deliberate now, in command of himself. This kind of thing would be an old story to him and the girl, reassured, put down the panic which the sight of that dust had brought. Her throat opened up. She breathed a bit more easily.

Maffitt *was* more himself now. That dust had served to settle his focus. Still pressed by his fears and ringed by doubts, here at least was something he could set his teeth into; he knew Casas' kind, had outguessed the man before and, now that he could see what he had to contend with, reckoned with luck he could do it again.

He wasn't fooling himself — it would be harder this time. Casas was sharp and proof of his shrewdness was in the changed slant of that dust back there; Casas was cutting over to intercept that trooper. He would lose perhaps a mile, maybe more, but he had already cut Maffitt's lead in half and, armed with what he would learn from that fellow, he would more than make up through their reversed positions any time lost in talking. Maffitt, in that set-to with the border patrol man, had put himself outside the law. There'd be no wraps on Casas this time. He'd be after a bonafide fugitive, in the right of things, and there was Katherin and that "marriage" to dig the spurs into him. And the remembrance of being made a fool of at Naco. Casas would be pulling no punches.

Nor would he be careless enough to let it be known it was the black stallion he was after. By the border man's tell of it the horse was suspect. Casas would have some plausible reason for being on their trail; Maffitt's trouble at McQuirchee's would give him pick of half a dozen. He would let on to being a Mexican national; the horses they were using would all be American branded. He might even be sporting a deputy's badge with credentials from Barr which, though without legal standing here, would get him courtesy and probably some measure of co-operation. Maffitt did not think it likely their dismounted friend would throw in with Casas to follow anyone across an international boundary, but the man might get a horse from him; once mounted he would lose no time getting Maffitt's description onto a wire.

There was no dust now. Casas, evidently, had come up with the trooper.

Maffitt stared ahead again. The mountains didn't look much nearer, but they were. He calculated those foothills he'd been heading for weren't far over four miles from Afligido's nose and it was two hours to dark. Studying their chances he pulled up to let the animals blow.

He scrubbed the sweat from his eyes and searched the terrain ahead more carefully. There were a lot of intangibles wrapped up in this business making it hard for a man to see his best chance, but one thing was sure — once Casas got his hands on them Maffitt's worries would be permanently cured.

Keeping his eyes grimly skinned for dust he pulled the saddles off the horses and, one at a time, let them roll. Then, since there was no grass here to amount to anything, he pulled off his shirt and rubbed one down while the girl walked the other. He knew better than to give them water. He did, however, hold the canteen out to the girl.

Katherin shook her head. "Better rinse your mouth out anyway," he said.

He would have stayed right here until dark had he dared; every confusion he could put in Casas' way would pay off in saved time and might ultimately spell the difference between continued health and its grim alternative. He didn't want Casas to know if he could help it at what precise point they'd be quitting this desert and if they could do it under cover of darkness they could gain more time than mere night itself would grant them. But Casas would see this, too.

Maffitt resaddled the horses, still absorbed with the prospects and what might be done with them. Casas would be a hard man to put off; it was even in the cards that he might know this country or have had sufficient acquaintance with it to outguess any reasonable move Maffitt made. Once dark came down to hide the fugitives' tracks he'd probably break up his party, pushing on with maybe half of them while the rest waited around for light to show them the trail. Before that — and this was certain, he'd come up with them if he could.

"They're coming," Katherin said and, peering west, Maffitt saw the dust.

"Wait —" he growled as, grasping reins and horn, she was about to swing up. He stood by the border man's appropriated mount, staring under his hand, narrowly watching, needing to gauge their pace, trying to determine the condition of the horses Casas had to work with. Like in every bunch there were a couple that were showing their heels to the rest, and it was a pretty safe assumption Chico Casas would be riding the foremost. That bunch was really moving now, pushing their broncs for all they were worth, determined to close with the fugitives, as Maffitt had foreseen, before night offered further chance to elude him. He'd know all about the condition of their stock.

To the girl it seemed as though Maffitt would never make up his mind. She felt a panicky urge to fling herself on the black and call for all the run he'd left in him. A glance at Maffitt's locked jaws held her fretting in her tracks. Watching that hateful dust boiling inexorably nearer and larger she tried in vain to still the pounding of her heart. Now she could hear even through and beyond it the dread sound of ground-gobbling hoofs drumming toward them. Afligido began sideling and shaking his head. Maffitt's horse caught the excitement; perhaps he smelled the fear in her. "All right," Maffitt said, and they swung up and got out of there.

It was maddening though the way he held the pace down. He wouldn't let either horse move out of a lope. Looking back she could mark Casas' big hat plainly, see the flap of his elbows and the ghostly strung-out shapes of the others behind him. She could see the light skitter off their big-rowled spurs, see the arms blurring wide with each swing of their quirts. Surely they weren't more than barely a mile away now . . .

They were nearer two, Maffitt judged, and the first fold of the hills were about equi-distant. He would let them get closer. He didn't know how they were armed but it would rub Casas harder to let them get a lot nearer before asking these horses for that final burst of speed. Be more likely to rob Casas too, and this was the point of it. There could be no one hurt until that bunch got close enough to start unlimbering blue whistlers.

He pulled his eyes to the front again. There was a canyon opening about a mile ahead of them, another one maybe half that far beyond. The second one, seeming narrower, looked to offer the better chance, he thought. The light wasn't good. The shadows racing ahead of them were more elongated now, looking like horsemen, not opaque like they had been, more of a gray kind of lavenderish substance that made them someway almost like real.

The sun, very quick now, would drop below the horizon. Dark would be on its heels. Be anybody's guess then where they had got to. If they could only hold Casas off a bit longer . . . Maffitt was sorely tempted to push the horses.

He peered over his shoulder. Casas' bunch were pretty widely strung out but Casas himself — Dale could see the big hat — and one other guy were getting awful close. He tried to measure their speed by things they were passing, the patches of stunted mesquite, the saguaros. The longer he could postpone disclosing his hand in the matter of his intentions the more likely he'd be able to carry them out. If they could let dark catch up with them . . .

He swept a glance at the girl. "Hold him in," he yelled. "Never mind that gulch," he called out on the heels of this, "Keep goin'!"

There was another crevice opening beyond the second one now and probably others farther along where the ground's rising contours were concealed in the thickening gloom. This new gash looked fairly promising, being closer to dark and displaying the bunched foliage of trees which could prove mighty useful if that bunch got to throwing lead.

Almost as though it had been spawned by the thought he caught the dim pulse of a sporadic popping that experience told him could only be guns. He knew without looking back that Casas anyway, and probably that other galoot, would be just about in range — long rifle range, anyhow. With the sun gone time was running out on Casas.

He'd be shooting for keeps, determined not to let them slip away from him again. This was Mexico. He could thumb his nose at Yankee law now, and memories of that chase south of Naco would be prodding him — likewise thoughts of the girl, who had also managed to make him look pretty silly.

Now was the time to find out what these horses could do. Casas must have remounted his crowd at McQuirchee's; himself, anyway, and that other fast mover.

Maffitt peered back at the muzzle winks. Still too far off to do much harm, he decided; and was twisting around to call for whatever their mounts could still give them when the front of his horse went down at one side, stumbling, going on through Maffitt's haul on the reins to stagger another final couple of strides and stop on three legs.

"*Goddam gophers!*" Maffitt snarled, sliding off.

10

Katherin was wheeling Afligido, swinging back with scared cheeks as Maffitt, face furious, jerked loose his Winchester. He laid the barrel across the stopped horse's saddle and, taking plenty of time with it, squeezed off a shot, worked the lever and tried another.

The lead horse, throwing its rider, went end over end with a scream that came dimly all the way up to them. The second horse staggered but kept on its feet to go wallowing off as the man sawed its reins in a frantic pull to the left. The spilled rider scrambled up without his big hat and Maffitt's stare narrowed. In this gray light the distance was too great to make anything of the blob of his features but he was plainly too short and too broad to be Casas. He broke into a run.

Katherin came up, slipping a foot from the stirrup. Maffitt stabbed a boot into it and, hanging onto his rifle — the only one they had, caught a hold on the horn and jumped himself up. "Let him out," he growled hoarsely.

The girl needed no urging. Lead was kicking up dust all about them and the big black, given his head, took off. Katherin crouched low across his outstretched neck. Maffitt, pressed close with his free arm around her, felt the whip of her hair against his cheeks. The clean, woman smell of it was in every rebellious breath he drew and — despite their peril and the confusions pounding through him — a heady lift like nothing he had known. He grew terrible conscious of the play of her muscles. There was no content in him, no least shred of satisfaction — only this bitter need she had unwittingly aroused and which he hated.

The gulch where he'd seen the trees was opening up ahead of them. He wanted now to pass it up, being still in sight of that bunch behind; but he dared not chance the black's legs, tired as he was and double burdened besides. There might be a lot of Steeldust or Traveler in his blood but this, by God, was no time to find out. What they needed right now was shelter. In all his reckoning he had not figured to be riding double. "Swing him in!" he cried and shifted weight.

The horse cut diagonally across the line of

fire. It was tricky going and Maffitt's heart stood still until a lift of tree-shrouded ground came between themselves and that racket of rifles. The air was cold against his sweat and he could feel the thud of the girl's frightened heart. "Keep him goin'!" he yelled, gripping hard with cramped knees.

It was spitting to windward, bawling it out like that and with them so near; but he was dealing, Maffitt figured, with a Latin kind of temperament that would have to pick and sniff like a hound. The bulk of that bunch would be border Mexicans expecting a cocked pistol back of each bush, a gringo trick in every move. Not even Casas would be immune to the duplicity he dealt in. Any notion you could plant in their heads which might tend to slow them down would be all to the good. Full dark was only minutes away and if he could make those minutes work for him he and the girl might get out of this yet.

The gulch was choked with brush and boulders. A man could ride a long way without coming onto a better spot, Maffitt reckoned; but he put temptation away from him. Holing up here was what they'd look for him to do — what they'd do in his place. They'd have all the best of it once those others got a chance to come up.

He let the black horse run just far enough to get out of sight. Then, reaching around the girl, Maffitt pulled up with a haul on the reins, sliding down over tucked tail to crouch listening. There was no close sound of hoofs but pretty soon he caught the guarded mutter of voices. Thinly grinning he took Afligido in tow and set off, with due care, to work a way out of this trap they were closing.

Patches of turf studded the ground here and there, grown and glued down through past runoffs, and as much as he could he kept to their quietness, avoiding the noisier stretches of gravel and all of the brush he was able to. They had to go through some, now and again, and he cursed it, thankful that Katherin at least kept her mouth shut. Every little while he stopped. Once he put an ear to the ground but heard nothing to indicate his ruse was discovered. That demonstration of what he could do with a rifle should keep them back for a little bit, anyway. Certainly that second hit bronc was in no shape to pack double and the first wouldn't be going no place at all.

The vague disquiet he'd felt when that fellow's hat came off was still gnawing him. The man who'd wheeled off hadn't been Casas, either. Of course Maffitt knew

nothing about Casas' courage; Chico probably believed in playing things safe, keeping
back out of gunfire till the quarry was down.
The thought didn't satisfy Maffitt, but there
wasn't time in this jackpot to worry it out
now; and he still had the girl on his mind,
and the danger.

This was still very real.

They were a long way from being out of
the woods by any measure — out of this
gulch, at any rate. Suppose it pinched out or
became impassable: The piled clouds he'd
seen, peering back in the sunset, had given
him hope they might get a little rain. A good
rain would wash out their tracks if they
could rebuild a lead. Scowling around at the
narrowing walls on both sides of him did
nothing to inspire any optimism, nor did he
care for what he could see of the rimrock.
This gulch was getting deeper; there was no
uptrend to the floor of it at all.

Maybe there was more than method in
the way those rannies were hanging back.
They might only be waiting for Casas or
they might know they had him bottled with
all the time in the world to come after him.

If it came to the worst Maffitt reckoned
they could probably manage to climb out on
foot but he hated to think of having to
abandon Afligido. By God, he'd no inten-

tion of letting that horse get back into their hands! If he'd only been alone in this deal . . . but wishing was like Pete Spence had said one time, more you did of it the more you needed. Pete was a small-time gambler who had jumped claims better than he'd dealt the bank. His whole damned life had been a series of wishes but about all they ever did for him was get him into trouble.

You could bury your head but facts stayed facts and when you got up you would have to run into them. Except for the girl he wouldn't be in this bind, but he was in it and she was with him. She was the albatross hung round his neck and no matter how fast or far a man traveled he could never run away from the sharp knife of conscience. It made no difference how the girl had got into this. It was up to him to look out for her. Regardless.

In fifteen minutes the gulch walls had pinched in to where the girl had to walk to get Afligido through, the passage simply wasn't wide enough with her legs about the horse; Maffitt had to loop the stirrups over the horn. It was so black in this slot he had to feel his way by touch and only kept on because he couldn't turn back. Twice the barrel of his Winchester clattered against the rough rock, sounding monstrously loud and carrying, he felt sure, halfway to El Paso. Once Afligido pulled back on the reins to nicker.

The shirt was stuck to Maffitt's back when, contrary to his dour expectations, the slot after a pair of sharp twists began to widen. Katherin was able once more to climb into the saddle. Within ten minutes the walls stood twenty feet apart and Maffitt's hopes began to rise. He stopped to listen again and heard no sounds at all behind.

"Do you think we've lost them?" Katherin presently asked. Maffitt grunted a negative, not bothering to enlarge on it. Those buggers knew where they were, all right; he could only hope this was all they knew.

He kept turning it over, attempting to evaluate every possible angle, but a man couldn't plan very far ahead when he didn't know jump from sic 'em. If any of that crew was familiar with this country he might be diving right out of the pan into the fire. Back there where they'd first come into this gulch he might have stood them off, at least for a little bit. If they could get in front of him and pick their time they might knock him down like a setting hen. Not seeing anything he could do about it there wasn't much choice but to push ahead. Some of that bunch were sure as hell coming after them. They wouldn't worry about tracks; he had lost that chance when they saw him duck into this. There was no other way for him to go with the girl.

Or without her, either, near as he could tell. These walls weren't as sheer as they had been but they still looked almighty steep and in this dark none but a fool would ever think of getting over them.

He had a new worry gnawing at him before they'd gone much farther. The floor of the gulch was here beginning to climb but there were no stars showing and the wind was getting up in a way he didn't like the sound of. He caught the distant growl of thunder and, abandoning caution, tried to step up their pace. He knew what these mountain storms could be like and he'd as soon get shot and be done with it as be trapped in this kind of place during a cloudburst.

The goddam boots were killing him by inches and in his hurry to get onto higher ground he tripped and went down three times in half a mile. He wrenched a leg in that third fall and it shook more than just a little caution back into him. If this climb lamed Afligido they might as well throw in their chips and give up.

Walking was purest agony now but he kept right ahead with it. The wind blew harder and had a cold dank feel to it that got clean into the marrow of his bones. The thunder came nearer, got a heap more scary, and the gulch began to flicker to the flare of distant lightning.

But the girl was chilled as he was and likely just as close to panic. Maffitt locked his chattering teeth and put more length in his stride, the black horse panting at the sharpness of the climb.

The gulch went into a series of twists. There was water under foot and minutes later, rounding a bend, rain struck down, lashing at them, blinding them. They had no defense against it and Maffitt and the black were soon ankle-deep in run-off. Both of them were gasping. In this treacherous footing travel was reduced to a snail's pace; every buffeting gust of the wind shook and pummeled them. Maffitt no longer looked ahead in his mind; all he looked for now was some place to get out of this, and there was no place. These walls were sheer granite.

11

At Bridle Bit there hadn't been a good rain in so long the oldest frog had chucked away his goggles and the last few crops had come along without webs. That Breeding's stock was in good shape where his neighbors' in the aggregate didn't show enough tallow to chink the ribs of a seam squirrel was largely due to the industry and foresight of Old Man Maffitt who, despite scandalized friends and the scurrilous comments of those who predicted him a pauper's grave, had poured every cent he could seize or borrow into drilled wells and ditching. He'd been a man too far ahead of his times and this publicized folly was paying real dividends to the partner whose expenditures had hung around his neck.

Breeding couldn't think where the fall had got to. It was still unseasonably warm, even for this mid-southern end of Arizona, but Christmas was only two weeks away and for the past several days the ranch had been swarming with activity, all hands working long and late, getting their first string ready for the races. You could pretty nearly always find people with more dollars than sense around Tucson, but Breeding had discovered that some of those towns over in Texas would bet even the pots that were under their beds anytime an outsider dared challenge one of their favorites. He had built this failing into a pretty good thing.

Months ago he had got his plans all lined up for this tour into Lone Star pockets. Down in South Texas over around the brasada — the big brush country — they had some pretty fast stock which he had no intention of coming anywhere near. He had fast stock himself, plus brains; which combination had led him to select Tatum, Midland, Rock Springs and Round Creek as the principal stages for his "get well" program. He'd be gone all winter with three of his saltiest hands, his chore boy and Heck Briggs, the wedge-faced jock who'd been ruled off at Chicago. Breeding would ship to the handiest points by rail.

Round Creek, because it was nearest and afforded the best possibilities, would be their first stop. They had a horse over there which was proclaimed unbeatable. He had found out more about that nag — a bay

137

called Snake Stomper, by Hearn's Yellow Jacket out of a mare by Brent's Traveler — than the packing house man who owned him had discovered in sixteen races. Breeding had been in touch, cash in hand, with all six of the animal's previous owners and his segundo, Vechel Harris, had talked with just about every fellow who ever had taken a run at the horse. Round Creek, Breeding figured, would put him on Easy Street.

He aimed to be there for Christmas.

It was some consolation — but not very much — to know that Casas, back of them someplace, would be just as bitterly furious with this unseasonable storm as Maffitt. Rain would wash out any sign they might leave but this appeared of dubious value to Katherin when, by the swiftness with which this water was rising, it might just as like wash them out along with it.

She'd seen enough of the damage caused by flash floods to have a very real fear of what they might be in for. In a matter of moments this gulch could become a millrace. Unless they could some way get off the floor of it . . .

She felt guiltily wicked and had the wild thought this whole thing came as punishment for the way she'd used Maffitt. She felt a need to make it up to him; but mostly she rode in a kind of beat numbness, in shivering despair, incapable of thought in any kind of coherence. Cold and shaking with the sodden rags plastered to her, half drowned already, gasping for breath, she clung to the saddle as the one solid thing in a world that was slipping away from her. Neither saddle nor horse nor even Maffitt — tough as he was — could stop a wall of water. Only God or chance could help them now. In this new humility she discovered her smallness, her complete unimportance; she prayed, dreading the roar that must herald their doom.

Maffitt, too, had his ears skinned but he wasn't counting the deal lost yet. They still had the rope that was on the black's saddle if he could find anything to dab its loop to. He knew of course in this kind of gale, in this savage ferocity of down-slashing rain, the cleverest hand was not likely to latch onto anything. He kept his mind away from that. He had to find a way. He hadn't prayed since he was a kid but he prayed now — not for himself but for the girl. God, take care of her, he growled, and felt he ought to say more but the words stuck in his throat.

And then it was too late. The sound he'd been expecting was suddenly all around them — even through wind and rain, through tumult of crashing thunder, he could hear it bouncing off the drenched rock surfaces like the boom and rumble of a mighty falls. High water!

No time to reach for rope, no place to go nor chance to get there if there had been. Maffitt grabbed the black stallion's cheek strap, fighting to keep the horse faced into it. Lightning ripped the night apart like the Hand of God jerking back a blanket. For an awful instant the roaring water stood revealed — solid, foam-frothed, towering over them, logs and bits of brush thrusting out of it like plumage in a red man's warlock.

Even as they stared, aghast, it was onto them, snatching Maffitt up like straw in a gale, whirling and pounding him, spinning him end over end, tumbling him through a rushing blackness where he had no control of himself at all, no way to fight back and nothing to fight with save a rebellious mind that stood off mouthing curses, strangely like Jonah in the belly of the whale. Half strangled, gasping in this spinning craziness he tried to fling himself up, get his head above surface. Something slammed into his side jerking his mouth open. Gagging he clutched the thing, hugging it to him, clinging with all his terrified strength, feeling the ungiving solidness of it, sensing its roughness, its frantic rush toward oblivion.

Twice his booted feet hit bottom and once he got his head out of water but he might as well have tried to hold back an avalanche as to curb the pace of that flood-gripped log. He dared not let go. This wasn't really a log; he knew that. More like a snapped-off section of tree trunk, the shattered stubs of thick branches still sticking out of it. Lungs about to burst he got a leg over one of these and, again for brief moments, found mouth and nose above surface. Gagging, gasping, he gulped precious air. He had a terrifying glimpse of the girl's fear-twisted face with the wet hair twined about it and, never knowing this was only in his head, cried out.

Roaring water churned and beat at him, wrenching, tearing at him like the grip of clawing fingers, pummeling and pounding him, jerking the log almost out of his grasp, lifting it and snatching it, the boil of mad currents sucking it down until one end, striking bottom, sent it booming toward the night again, spewing it forth like a retch from sour stomach.

Pain, knifing through Maffitt's back, convulsed him, emptying the breath from his burning chest, threatening paralysis, blacking out thought. He felt salvation slipping away from him or maybe it was his hands falling away from the rolling trunk. With a last spurt of strength he wildly clutched for it . . .

He was never afterwards able to recall what happened for a while then, nor could he imagine how long or to what extent he was out of touch with things. He supposed he lost consciousness. More likely he regained his hold. Although the racket of furious water still rang in his pounding ears the next thing he felt for certain was a sense of uncaring lassitude, a complete cessation of movement. He seemed to have fallen into a vacuum.

Memory suddenly caught up with him, jerking open his eyes to the star-filled night, to the thunderous roar of still racing water and the black blocks of rock rimming him around like waiting vultures.

He grew conscious of a tugging at the ends of his legs and realized that the lower halfs of them were still in water. He came onto an elbow, groaning as pain splintered through him, and looking down, wondered that he had found either the wit or energy to haul himself even this far out of it. He had no remembrance of doing so.

He saw the girl then — saw, rather, the

white-swathed bentover shape of her, feeling the strike of her eyes, the frank concern that was in her as she pushed onto one knee and braced hands. He thought for an anxious moment those arms, so pitifully frail in this dark, were going to fold under her. They proved adequate in spite of her obvious exhaustion and he guessed then how he had gotten here.

They were on a piece of shingle, a sloping section of rock-littered sand, a kind of hollowed-out declivity in this nest of great boulders above a jam of interlocked trunks and branches which appeared to have formed a sort of dam. Some of that brush or mangled flotsam must have caught and held him and the girl must have dragged him out — he reckoned she must have. He could never have got over that mess without help.

He said, considerable chagrined at the puny sound of it, "You all right?"

She did not speak immediately, but nodded. "I suppose so . . . at least, I *guess* I'm all in one piece. Can you get up?"

"Don't know," he said, half afraid to try. He scowled at the water rushing through and over that wedged tangle of debris, scarcely able even yet to believe he had got out of it. "Seems incredible," he muttered.

Katherin shivered. "Must be thirty feet

deep right there, maybe more. It's slowed down a lot," she told him. "Not nearly so fierce as it was a couple hours ago. A bit lower, too — we're up on the rim of the south wall, I think. Do . . . do you suppose they'll give up and go back now?"

"Not Casas. Soon's the water gets out of this gulch —"

"But wouldn't he have been caught just as bad or maybe worse?"

"Not likely," Maffitt said. "He wasn't near as anxious to get into this place as we was. Maybe he never come into it at all." He pulled his feet from the water, clamping his jaws against the jagged searchings of pain coming out of his back and left side. He blackly hoped this was nothing more serious than bruised flesh; he couldn't afford any broken bones sticking out of his skin. Which was one blessing, anyhow.

"Are you sure you're all right?" The girl anxiously studied him.

Maffitt wasn't sure of anything beyond that both of them were still alive. It didn't seem possible they could have got out of that flood without sustaining anything more serious than a drenching. Luck was luck but he had seldom found cause to put any great faith in it. He was still feeling himself over when they heard a horse whicker.

The both of them stiffened, eyes cocked, afraid to move. The sound came again. "Afligido!" Katherin cried, and got shakily onto her feet. Maffitt, grimacing, pulled up his legs and tried to work off his boots. He had to give it up. He lay back and raised his legs, one at a time, letting some of the water run out. He tried to get up then. The girl had to help him. Except for pride and his own desperation he'd have dropped back down. Putting weight onto that hurt leg was very like pushing it into a fire. He had to fight back the nauseous giddiness that was making girl and ground spin about him.

When he could trust the words to come out right he said — and the sound of them fell quite a way short of pleasing him — "Where do you reckon he is?"

"Sounded to me as if he were somewhere north of us, maybe around the next bend." She studied him anxiously. "You wait here. I'll go look —"

"I'll take the look," he growled, shaking her hand off. It might not be Afligido at all. About one chance in twenty that it was, he thought. More likely to be one of Casas' crowd. That water may have carried them back a good piece. May have washed them right into Chico's ever-loving grip.

North, she'd said. That would be higher

into the mountains. He saw at once there'd be no going in that direction. Sheer rock and plenty of it, and that goddam rushing water. He wasn't about to take to that!

Peering across the girl's shoulder he thought he might be able to get off this shingle if he headed east. Might be a way around from there. He said again, "You stay right here," and went limping off between a pair of big stones that not even a Morgan horse could have budged. The girl didn't answer.

She didn't wait, either.

He glared at her when he heard the squish of her feet coming after him. "God damn it —"

"A wife's place," Katherin said, "is with her man."

Maffitt gave her a bitter look and went on. There was scraped hide along his left side and he could tell by the feel it was bleeding again. He reckoned his back had a gouge out of it too, but he guessed he'd live through it if they didn't run into Casas. Without guns and after the pounding he had taken from the river he could see well enough what chance they'd have if that happened. It was a chance he had to take. Without food and no shelter they were done for anyway unless they could get hold of that horse.

He was glad of the dark because it kept her from guessing how bad off they were. This was survival they were fighting for and no use kidding himself that it wasn't. The wind had laid but in these wet things the night seemed colder than a pair of dressed frogs legs. He could hear her teeth chattering. Walking was their only hope for the moment. He wasn't fretting about himself; he'd spend a lifetime getting used to feeling stove up.

There was a way up over the rim here. Treacherous going in the dark and middling steep too, but it seemed like they were going to make the rim. They did, and the wind he thought had died really hit them there. It had the feel of snow. Higher up there probably was snow. The thought made him clamp his jaws even tighter. If they got the horse they'd damn well head south pronto — Casas or no Casas. Nothing Casas could do would be much worse than freezing to death or dying of exposure. Like to be considerable quicker.

They crept along the rim, pointing as nearly north as this permitted, Maffitt straining to catch some sound from the horse, knowing that in this wind it wasn't likely. So far as he could tell the rim fell sheer to the right of them, no guessing how far but too far for comfort.

A fall the way they were now could be just as disastrous as stopping a slug. Katherin needed a fire and regardless of prudence he would have got one going if he'd had anything to make it with. The rain had quit but everything was sopping and pretty soon, if this wind kept up, it was going to be frozen — themselves included.

He tried to take comfort in reminding himself they might both have been drowned. They were still alive and had the use of their limbs. But aside from this he didn't see how they could have been in worse shape. They were, of course, still free of Casas — for the moment.

It wasn't too likely the man would find their tracks. Not up here, anyway; and it would be several hours before the gulch offered passage to anything short of a boat. If they, or the law, hadn't got this far in advance of the storm . . . But that was the hitch; he didn't know that they hadn't. He didn't see how he was going to find that horse, either. *God, but it was cold!*

His eyes kept searching the windy dark. He wanted to run, to get them into better cover, but he was bound to this rim until he could find another break in the spine of rock that would let them drop back toward the water. He dared go no faster; one misstep could easily prove fatal. He cautioned the girl time and again, he even took her hand over some of the worst places. Hope began to frazzle out of him. Pain was like a saw working in him. He had about abandoned even thinking of getting clear when the horse whinnied again somewhere below and to the left of them.

The sound was pretty faint. He was afraid at first he'd imagined it, was about to push on when Katherin caught at his arm. "Wait — I think we've gone past."

She might be right. He thought of calling to the horse on the chance it might call back, but was afraid to, remembering Casas. The girl huddled against him, clinging to him, shaking. He knew he had to get her out of this wind. He threw his voice toward the gulch. The horse answered and it *was* Afligido! Maffitt was sure now. "Come on," he growled, and began to look for a way down, examining with eyes and hands each slant and crevice. Soon, within rods, they were scrambling down but he knew, even as they did so, he was not going to get any horse over this. They'd have to find another way and if there wasn't one . . . He pulled his mind away from that. At least they'd be out of the worst of this wind.

He heard the horse again, the squishy stomp of its hoofs to the left of them someplace. Holding the girl's arm Maffitt cut over that way, not saying anything but dreading what they might find. If the horse was stove up . . .

The stallion wasn't. He was trapped on a piece of shingle very similar to the one Maffitt and Katherin had quit. This was larger, rimmed with rock as their own had been, its single outlet hard against the water and blocked with the branches of a stunted half-dead juniper. They had to tear their way through these to get to him. Maffitt wasn't at all sure they could get him out, but his first concern was to make certain the horse was able.

So far as they could tell there was nothing wrong with his legs that time and nature would not take care of. He was pretty well skinned up with a nasty-looking gash across one hip. The girl kept rubbing him, making little crooning sounds while Maffitt went over him as well as he could. That gash was the worst thing; it appeared more serious than it actually was. There was a bad scrape on one leg but it was just hide that was missing. Maffitt left them talking to each other and, wrenching up a stone — egg-shaped and somewhat larger than a football

— commenced battering the gnarled branches. Ten minutes of this and he had to rest without having made any great amount of headway. He had smashed off some of the branches but there was nothing like enough room for the horse.

Maffitt threw down the rock. Afligido still had his saddle and the rope Dale had taken from the snake-bit grulla was still buckled to it, twisted and tangled. The question was how to make use of it. He picked up the rock and began pounding at an exposed root that went into the ledge below those stumps of broken branches. The root was thick around as the upper half of Maffitt's arm, and mostly dead but still tough. He finally got up and dropped the rock on it; it bounced over the edge and went into the water.

But it had made an impression. Maffitt got another, bigger one.

Drenched with sweat and panting he went over and started untwisting the rope. There wasn't a whole lot he could do with it. Taking the end that wasn't hitched to the saddle horn he went back to the juniper and, gouging out some of the muck under the root, slipped the rope through and hitched it. Katherin, realizing his intention, had fetched the horse up. Maffitt tightened the cinches but couldn't get aboard. The girl, watching narrowly, said, "Dale, you're hurt —"

"Just that damn leg. I can't put enough weight on it."

"I'll back him," she said. Her feet had taken a beating on those rocks. The one she lifted must have been half numb; she had to use a hand to get it into the stirrup. She hauled herself up. "Back him easy now," Maffitt said, unkinking the rope as well as he could. "All right — steady, now."

The rope stretched and sang. "Watch out," he called, worried. "If that damn string snaps —"

It did, right then, the length that was tied to the saddle coming speed-blurred back like the strike of a snake. But the horse, shaken out of braced stance by its parting, had moved enough that Katherin — though gasping — was not particularly hurt. She had a welt along one thigh where that white thing she had on had not altogether covered her. She might have lost an eye.

Maffitt took the frayed end and she moved Afligido up as he went back with it. She realized then how much thinner the dark had got; it was almost day. Maffitt, bent over the root, straightened, grunting. "Try it again — easy now."

Popping sounds came from the twisting

root. "Easy!" Maffitt growled. The hitch being shorter, the pull this time was more direct and from a different angle. The saddle creaked, the rope went taut as a piece of stretched gut. Maffitt pushed a hand out. She held Afligido steady while he bent for another look. "We're gettin' it," he said. "A little more now."

The ground was breaking, pushing up all around it. Four feet of scraped root came out of the ledge with a rush and she slacked the horse off as the broken end popped into sight. Maffitt limped up and pried the tied rope off the horn and, not wanting to get tangled up in it, threw it into the water which was now six feet below the level of the shelf. He got his back against the ledge and, bracing his good leg against the bole of the tree, put all the strength he could into the push. She could see the white vapor of his breath in this cold.

Sweat stood out on his whiskered face. The tree gave a little, its groans almost human. Something snapped and the trunk leaned outward, creaking, over the growl of muddy water. Lower it tipped and lower still. Maffitt came away from the ledge and catching hold of the upthrust root pushed it over.

There was hope on Katherin's pinched

cheeks again. "Stay aboard," Maffitt panted as she would have got down. She brought the black up and he snorted, eyeing distrustfully the torn-up ground, shaking his head at it, sideling nervously. Maffitt picked up the short length of broken rope that had been lapped about the root and, fashioning a hackamore, slipped it over the stallion's head. Talking to him, soothing him, Maffitt led them out of the pocket.

The eastern sky was streaked with pink and rose. They had no trouble seeing where they were going. Maffitt's limp was no worse and the bite of his pain was less noticeable now, though every bone and muscle ached as if he'd just been loosed from a rack. He'd have given considerable for some liniment right then and dry clothes for the girl — a bite of food if he could get them, but would have settled for much less and had no hope of anything. They'd be lucky indeed if they were able to reach shelter. It was so cold, Maffitt's teeth, despite these recent exertions, would have chattered like castanets if he had dared unclamp his jaws. But there was confidence in Katherin's eyes again and maybe she was right, maybe their luck would change. They had at least gotten rid of Casas for awhile.

He found a way up onto the rim that

Afligido could negotiate and, half an eternity later, a talus slope along its eastern flank let them down into lower country across a wooded plateau that kept a lot of wind off them. When they came out of the trees they saw snow high up on the towering peaks. The wind got at them again but their clothes were about dry now and the sun, bounding over the broken country ahead of them, was a welcome sight.

They were still cold, half numb — even Maffitt — and as they dipped still lower into the trough of a valley, hunger began to get in its licks: he wondered how much longer he could stay on his feet. They could have taken turns with the horse — might have done that yesterday, not withstanding the heat, if she'd had any shoes. Now, when such exercise might have helped warm her, it was again her feet which kept him on his.

He was mightily tempted to get on Afligido with her but something in the back of his head wouldn't let him. Seemed like she was talking or making out to talk, rambling on about what she had thought or done or the river had done to her when she'd been in that water, but he couldn't make heads nor tails of it. There were stretches through here which he had considerable trouble with on account of the way the damn ground kept pitching. Sometimes the pear clumps and cholla seemed to be growing right out of the sky but he wouldn't let this bother him, knowing how mirages could fool a man. His feet didn't seem to have any more feeling than a bunch of crumpled-up paper and he reckoned this was one of them blessings to be counted but he sure as hell wished they weren't so god-dam heavy.

He lost all track of time. Got so he couldn't hardly tell one ridge from the next or if he was going downhill or crossways but, whenever he thought of it, he looked at his shadow; it was the only thing he had that he could for sure set any course by. Spite of all that he could do it kept edging around to the left of him and finally got so contrary it tried to run ahead of him. He wasn't going to stand for that; he wasn't about to.

He never did get the straight of how he got there but when he presently was jolted out of whatever it was that was ailing him he was astonished to find himself aboard Afligido — in the saddle by God, but the hand that was holding the shank of the stallion's halter rope didn't look like either of the ones he was used to — didn't look like it belonged to him at all. Kind of reminded him someway of Katherin's.

Then he noticed something else. Afligido was stopped with a clutter of buildings strung out ahead of them — shacks these was really, the most of them coming apart at the seams or about to. And there was a mob of people round him with their eyes big as slop buckets and one of them, a great gaunt stick of a jigger in a chin-strapped hat that wouldn't of gone through one of them doors, was reaching up a fist to get hold of . . . It was the look of that face that knocked the breath out of Maffitt.

Though he found it hard to believe, the man standing back of that grin was Casas.

12

Katherin, too, had seen that grinning face, had discovered and recognized it well in advance of Maffitt, before the crowd blocked Afligido. Spurred by shock and consternation each frantic instinct had pushed her toward flight, but the condition of the stallion — even if she could have jettisoned Maffitt, told her flight was out of the question.

She'd sensed at once what must have happened. The steepled hats she and Maffitt had seen had fooled them into imagining it was Casas back of them whereas it must have been part of a posse. The hats had covered only a couple of Casas' bravos he must have talked her dad into taking, probably bragging them up as expert trackers. The man had either outguessed them right at the start or had picked up knowledge which had put him into the mountains ahead of them. It did not matter how he happened to be here, the fact of his presence was more than adequate.

Working the ring off her finger she knew a trapped and terrible sense of frustration — and fear — as the crowd closed around them. Casas was a cat with a plateload of salmon and you could tell by his eyes he hadn't forgotten or forgiven anything. Maffitt, in the leather, in front of her, had apparently not remembered they were both without weapons; he jabbed a hand at his empty holster.

Casas threw back in a loud hoot of derision and Maffitt's good leg, lashing forward, slammed a boot against the side of his face, sending him sprawling. Maffitt jerked Afligido's head about but a dozen reaching hands caught and stopped the horse before he'd gone two jumps and Casas, scrambling up, hauled Maffitt out of the saddle and clouted him twice across the face with his pistol.

Maffitt reeled and with blood running down his cut cheeks tried to grapple. Casas kicked him in the groin. As Maffitt doubled in agony Casas clubbed him with the pistol, struck again with vicious fury. Maffitt dropped. Katherin, finding no help in that sea of avid faces, fought down her panic, stifling the cry that would have betrayed her. "Chico — Chico," she called hoarsely —

"thank Heaven!" and, dropping off the black, ran to him, throwing her arms around him.

The Mexican, looking a little bug-eyed, shoved her away. She would have stumbled had the crowd not been pressed so close about. Her cheeks went pale and she gasped, bewildered. "You — surely you don't believe I . . ." and let the rest go, put all the considerable ability she had into a regard which considered him in stricken amazement.

Casas would not have been Casas had he honestly believed any woman in her right mind would voluntarily have run off with this gringo dog in preference to himself, but he'd sustained some bad jolts in these past few days and in his present temper would have distrusted the archangel Gabriel. Ignoring her, he stood over the prostrate gringo and deliberately, furiously, kicked him in the head and ribs, each brutal impact bringing a whimpering groan from Maffitt.

It wasn't pity or shame that made the Mexican, panting, finally step back to stand glowering down upon the no longer conscious object of these attentions. He wanted Maffitt to know what was happening to him; he wanted it to hurt but he had a more exquisite punishment in store which he meant the gringo to be in shape to appreciate.

Some of this showed in Casas' face. He waved an arrogant hand. One of the mule men ran off and came back with a bucket of water which he splashed over Maffitt. Two others dragged him onto his feet and when his eyes began to focus Casas spat in his face.

Katherin watched the spittle run down his torn cheek. "Good!" she cried in a voice that cracked. Hobbling over to stand on bleeding feet beside Casas she too spat on Maffitt and, with the crowd scarcely breathing, eyeing him contemptuously she said with curling lips, "Let me see you laugh now! Let me hear you brag how smart you are in front of this man you said couldn't catch a blind duck with one wing off!" She spat on him again and started pounding him with her fists.

Casas dragged her away. "Enough!" he growled, grinning across her shoulder at Maffitt's bitter face. "You shall have your chance at this dog, never fear." He barked a sharp command and the pair who had hold of Maffitt hurried him off somewhere out of her sight.

"Come, chiquita," Casas said, gripping her elbow. He hawked up some words in rapid Spanish and a wrinkle faced crone with a black shawl over her wispy hair and shrunken shoulders scurried ahead of them.

The Mexican kept a firm hand at Katherin's elbow but it seemed to the anguished girl this was more in the nature of constraint than with any idea of helping her. She couldn't tell if her treatment of Maffitt had fooled him; she was filled with dread and it was all she could do in the face of their prospects to keep up the part she had elected to play. She knew, revolted, that she must, but her tongue was dumb. One wrong word now, one visible shudder, would destroy the last slim chance they had. For the moment, anyway, Maffitt was helpless, could do nothing by himself. He had to have rest, a chance to gain strength and get hold of himself. The posse . . . She pushed that away from her. There was little chance of the posse overtaking them now.

Casas, still retaining his hold, moved her after the old woman to a box-like hovel of unplastered adobe, shoving her roughly through the held-open door. The old woman went away.

The Mexican, lounging against the jamb, considered her inscrutably. She felt the heat come into her cheeks, saw the thin twist of grin that briefly showed at his lips. "Clean yourself up," he said gruffly. "You'll find clothes back of that curtain — the old one's whelp is near enough to your size."

He backed out, still with that half feral glint in his stare. "Refresh yourself. Sleep. You'll not be bothered if you keep out of sight. Tomorrow —"

She said, eyes flashing, "When you do whatever you're going to with him . . ."

"You will be there, rest assured. I will see you tomorrow," Casas promised, and shut the door.

She listened to the departing crunch of his boots. She didn't like the way he had looked at her or the twist of that grin. Her glance swept the room — there was only one, kept as clean as vigilance and broomweed could make it. The floor was of dirt, hard packed from countless sprinklings. Except for a crucifix over the bed the walls were bare. There was one wired-together straightback chair somewhat short of rungs and a dilapidated bureau with a wavy glass and a curtain of cheap print across one angle of the walls; there was a tiny fire of mesquite wood in mound of baked mud on the triangular platform of adobe bricks in the corner opposite the curtain. Katherin stretched shaking hands to the blaze.

She had got the man into this; it was up to her to give Maffitt a chance, but fear was a

knife twisting deep in her now. She shook
uncontrollably. She could not put from her
mind the look of Casas' eyes so enigmati-
cally watching her. She had never learned
what business the man had with her father
but she remembered what that border patrolman had said about guns and the black
Afligido and had little doubt this was what
had been back of it. Her father, as sheriff,
could be useful . . .

But her thoughts kept harking back to
Casas, to the scary look that had been in his
eyes. Here he could do whatever he wished
with her . . . these were poor people, mule-
teers, wood gatherers; some of them probably out-and-out bandits. Casas was a rico,
the strong right hand of his excellency the
Governor, General Olivares.

She cringed, remembering stories she had
heard. There would be no further talk of
marriage. It would be every night and most
of the night . . .

She had to distract herself. She went to
the curtain and peering back of it saw a
boarded-over crate with a cracked crockery
basin and chipped pitcher half filled with
clean water. An orange skirt full of pleats
and a grass-green blouse or camisa hung
from a peg and, from a second, a black low-
cut satin gown with red insets and trim. Like

the pitcher and basin of glazed crockery these seemed out of place in such surroundings until she recalled Casas' mention of the old lady's "whelp." She understood then what these were the fruits of, and shivered.

She had to face it. Condemnation, vindictive talk about Maffitt would never be enough. If she would give Maffitt any real help she must appear to look forward to . . . she must appear to encourage Casas. If necessary she must be prepared to . . . *Father God, give me strength.*

She carried the pitcher and basin over by the fire that barely warmed this room and worked on her feet, afterwards wrapping them in strips torn from one of her flood-wrinkled underskirts, trying not to think, to put the future away from her.

She went and sat in the chair, determined no matter what to keep away from the bed. But the chair was hard, the flesh is weak and she had been through enough to overwhelm almost anyone. She kept fighting to stay awake, afraid to give in to the exhaustion which claimed her, afraid of the door which there was no way to fasten. Afraid . . .

She kept nodding, kept jerking frantically awake. Where was the old woman — the girl who owned the bright clothes in the corner? Had Casas put them out of their house? She got up and moved around, found cold beans, a crust of bread, and ate these, suddenly ravenous. She found it next to impossible to keep her eyes open. She dragged the packing case out of the curtained corner and wedged it best as she could against the door. There was just the one window; she got the curtain off its rope and covered the black and glistening glass. She stared a long while at the bed and finally, because she was cold and couldn't hold her eyes open, pulled down the patched scrubbed-thin blanket and, still wearing all the river had left her, got into it.

The adobe they shut Maffitt up in had no windows, no eyes but the loopholes cut into it for rifles, and only one door which was as massively solid as a stockade gate. Even so, they left him tied hand and foot, flat on his back on a table in its center. During those brief periods when his mind erratically functioned he could hear someone stamping around outside and correctly assumed this was a guard posted to make certain no one tampered with him.

A long time later he came awake to somebody shaking him. The door was open and by the wan light this let in he saw the face of an old man peering down. This ancient untied him and stood back, narrowly watching, while Maffitt rubbed circulation back into limbs that seemed stuck full of pins and needles. He couldn't at first even sit up by himself; the old man kept away from him, answering his questions with enigmatic grunts. Maffitt wondered if he were dumb until the man said finally, "You walk now?"

Maffitt got gingerly off the table. His wrenched leg was considerably better, but stiff; and when he tried to walk both legs doubled under him. When he pulled himself up it took almost five minutes of flexing and stamping to get enough life back into them to use them. This was when he discovered the second man standing back in the shadows with a lifted rifle. The old man put a tin pan filled with food on the table and under their watchful eyes Maffitt ate. When they motioned him outside, pointing out a privy, he saw a third man similarly armed, a part-Yaqui, eyeing him through a tangle of uncombed black hair. He saw by the sky that it was almost night but knew by his condition it was not the same day he'd stumbled into this trap. All the while he was in the backhouse the pair who had accompanied him stood outside the door, neither one of them speaking. It was plain enough to Maffitt that Casas had this village eating out of his hand.

He started back, thoughts whirling wildly. Both men fell in behind him. The light was poor, deceptive for shooting. He let his shoulders sag. He stumbled, staggered, caught himself and shambled on. The third man, smoking a black cigarillo, had his rifle, unaimed, in the crook of an arm with his back against the wall perhaps three yards to the right of the door. He had a stupid-looking face.

Maffitt, head bent to go through the door, abruptly spun, hurling himself into the gun-bearer back of him. The man cried out, trying to get up his rifle. Maffitt, twisting it out of his hands, knocked him into the old man, throwing both of them off balance. He had the weapon up then, gripped by the barrel, and was starting a scythe-like swing when the world fell in on him, hammering him down with the roar of an avalanche.

When he came to again he was back on the table. The door was shut. The old man and the Yaqui were playing some kind of a card game with colored pebbles for stakes in the flickering light of a cow-fat candle. His head felt like a mule's heel had hit it.

Sounds of someone trying to force the door brought Katherin wide awake with a rush. "Tortillas, enchiladas, frijoles y chili."

It was the old woman's voice. There was sunlight, pinkish and pale, against the curtain Katherin had hung across the window and the room was filled with shadows. The girl, suddenly famished, got stiffly up and, hobbling across the cold earthen floor, dragged the box away from the door. The old woman reached in, put the plate of food down and, with an inscrutable glance from eyes black as malpais, went away.

Katherin said "Damn!" into the white whorl of her breath and, shivering, took the plate over to the cold hearth then pushed the box back against the door. If anyone really aimed to get in this wouldn't keep them out but at least it would give her warning. She found the slop jar under the bed. She took it out back, there finding a small store of cut wood which she fetched in.

She built up a fire, washed, ate, doing her best to keep her mind under wraps without great success. Very soon she was going to have to face up to what Chico Casas had in store for her; this realization alone was enough to blunt her appetite. She got shaking again. She told herself hysteria would not help her. Neither could Maffitt. She had a guilty feeling about Maffitt. Of course there was the horse, but at least a part of Casas' fury was directed at

Maffitt because of her.

She set about improving her appearance. When she'd done all she could she put more wood on the fire. She couldn't get warm and shook as with an ague. It wasn't chills and fever; it was Casas that so unnerved her. She had only her wits to rely on now. She might, and with reason, pretend to be ill. But nothing, she knew, was in the long run going to stand in his way. This was Mexico. Casas was a big man and while some of these people might not see eye to eye with him she couldn't picture any of them openly opposing him. Why should they? She was nothing to them, nor was Maffitt. They had their own problems. Death and desire were facts of life around here, common denominators. Accepted as such. You had to realize these people were conditioned to abuse.

She must have remained awake past midnight but Chico Casas did not come.

She was up again at first crack of day. She washed, made the bed and in her mind, time after time, went repeatedly over the whole unsavory business without noticeably improving her prospects. It all boiled down to Casas, a man of pride and spirit. She had, in a way, made a fool of him, as had Maffitt; the man would never let this pass. His own queer perception of honor would demand retribution; at the very least there'd be a wall for Maffitt, a bed for Sheriff Barr's daughter. These were the inescapable summations of her thinking. Whether or not she succeeded in misleading the Mexican there'd be a bed at the end of it. Beds and Casas went together like ham and eggs.

She built up the fire — at least she didn't have to freeze. She brought in the last of the wood, put the colorful blouse and skirt on over her own bedraggled underthings and, with sinking heart, pulled the box aside when a crunch of steps came over the frozen ground to stop outside the door.

But it was not Casas. It was a girl with her breakfast. Not so tall as Katherin, black-haired and strikingly handsome despite, or perhaps because of, that odd slant of eye and rebelliously, sullen mouth. Lithe, full-breasted and hatefully bold in the hostile way her angry gaze jabbed at Katherin as she put down the food and jug of coffee she had brought.

Katherin backed off a little, not afraid but watchfully wary.

Scorn flashed out of the girl's dark glance and she pulled back her shoulders. "I am Rosa. You want go from thees place? I get you horse."

"Where is Casas?"

She could almost taste the other girl's reaction. The agate eyes burned with hate, the thin nostrils dilated. "Casas mine — same those clothes, this house!"

Understanding came to Katherin; she almost smiled at the absurdity, the irony of this girl imagining . . . "I'm not after him," she said gently.

"You lie!" Rosa said fiercely. "Every woman want heem — *no le hace*. I get you horse. Good horse — fast."

Katherin was tempted. This was no trap, nothing Casas had put her up to. The girl was jealous, afraid of her. With a good horse . . . She shook her head.

"Afligido?" the girl said bitterly. "You go then, eh?"

"No."

They eyed each other across this taut stillness. Katherin could feel the desperation in Rosa. But it was Katherin's fault, much as it was anything, that Maffitt was where he was right now. She couldn't just ride off and leave him — and where would she go? Her self confidence was badly shaken; she didn't have Maffitt's experience, Maffitt's hard competence. A lone woman . . .

Glance thoughtfully widening she considered Rosa more carefully. The girl was wild to get rid of her; in her present state defi-

nitely dangerous, ready by the look of her
. . . Katherin said tentatively, "I am not
without means. I have money —"

"I spit on it!"

Katherin said patiently, "I'm not trying to
buy —"

"You not buy heem! You not get heem — I
keel!" Rosa cried, suddenly brandishing a
knife. All bowed up she came through the
door like the dart of a rope. "You go!" she
gritted through bright teeth, breasts
heaving.

Katherin backed away from that angry
glitter. "Wait — look! I can't go alone, he
would find me sure." Her mind was sharp.
"He's determined to marry me."

She told the lie baldly, figuring the girl, remembering that mention of money, would
find in it the real key to belief. Belief was all
Katherin wanted right now. She saw the
girl's altered look, the hesitant pause, and
prodded. "If you could get Maffitt free and
provide us with horses —"

"Mafeet?"

"The man who was with me. The one
Casas beat."

The black eyes darted over Katherin's
hands. "What is he to you, these Mafeet, eh?
You loffer?"

Katherin, flushing, was glad she'd had the

173

sense to get rid of that ring. She couldn't very well admit Maffitt was her husband — that she was already married. One facetious corner of her mind, however — even in this uncomfortable moment — had a vision of Maffitt being confronted with this status and the ludicrous thought of it tickled her mightily. She nodded more emphatically, hard put to keep a straight face.

But the expression of Rosa quickly sobered her. The black eyes were bright with distrust and suspicion. The girl was trying the blade of her knife with a thumb, her hard stare never blinking. Then another thought caught her; the black eyes narrowing craftily. "You pay?"

Katherin's nod was too ready, too visibly eager. All the doubt and dark suspicions came into Rosa's look again. Katherin, starting to reach for the purse, stopped, stiffly rigid, and then went on with it. Whatever came of this was out of her hands now. The money no longer mattered; getting away was all that counted. With Maffitt loose and both of them mounted she could put this place out of her mind, and Casas with it. Maffitt had lost the man once and could again.

"Please hurry!" she said, and held out the purse; but Rosa, turned wary, stayed away from her, catching it deftly when Katherin tossed. The Mexican girl opened it, watching her slanchways, poked around with a finger before tucking it into the cleft of her breasts. With a last, hating look she put away her knife and went off, not bothering to shut the door. Not saying anything, either.

Katherin worried. The hours dragged interminably. It was the longest day she had ever put in, gray and gloomy with a low rack of clouds shutting out the sun. But at last it was dusk, the depressing room filled with shadows. The old woman came with her supper, not talking, ignoring Katherin's questions about Casas. She stood by the door while Katherin ate, gathering up the dishes and carrying them away immediately after.

There were no candles in the house. Katherine built up the fire with the last of the wood. Restless and fretful she paced the cold floor in a pair of rope sandals she had found with the clothes. With each outside sound her forlorn hopes revived, becoming solid despair when the sounds without pausing faded out in the night. Rosa was laughing at her, hating and despising her. She was probably with Casas — but no, that didn't make sense; the girl was too obviously jealous and hostile. Wherever Casas was he was certainly not with Rosa.

Katherin had never imagined the girl would help them for the money but she had rather hoped the girl might do it to be rid of her. — The knife was sheerly bluff, of course — or was it? Rosa *might* be wild enough . . . She stiffened, intently listening.

It had been warmer today, the ground hadn't frozen. She was sure there'd been someone outside moving furtively. Yes! She's not been mistaken; someone was coming.

Trembling, she dragged aside the heavy crate, all thumbs in her excitement. She was filled with a sense of exultation in the heady thought that very soon now she'd be getting away from here; she'd handled that girl just right. This was Maffitt, of course. She pulled open the door and fell back, aghast.

Casas, darkly grinning, stepped into the room.

13

Katherin was too unnerved to speak.

Her feet seemed lost but even through shock the flame of the man's feral stare fetched her legs alive and she moved, in a kind of stringhalted jerkiness, deeper into the room until the backs of her knees came against the bed, trapping her.

In sudden desperation she tried to dart past. His jabbed-out arm was too quick. Spread fingers sank into her shoulder like hooks. Momentum carried her half around, legs tangled, like a calf hitting the end of a rope.

Casas, hugely enjoying every bit of it, laughed, the sound gurgling up from deep in his throat. The painful grip tightened. His free hand came out like the paw of a bear, with terrible ease ripping the blouse and all under from neck to belly in one savage yank. Katherin's heavy breasts spilled into full sight in her frantic attempts to wrench free of his grip. The pant of their breathing grew loud in the room and he was forced back a step, whipped and swayed by her struggles, but his grip was like steel; she couldn't get loose of it.

His eyes drove her crazy; she bit, stamped and kicked. He laughed at her fury. She got her nails into his face, tried to get at his eyes. He cuffed her, making her head ring. The room whirled and, next thing she knew, she was on the bed, all the breath shaken out of her.

Her bulging eyes found him then, looming monstrously over her, grinning out of that bloody mask, a belt in his hand and the hand slicing out and up in the move that would bring the flap end of it whistling down onto her.

Her flesh cringed. She brought up both arms but the blow didn't fall. Casas' towering shape was suddenly, rigidly, still, all the corrugations of his face grotesquely frozen. Katherin stared, not understanding, not able to move until her startled eyes took in the shadow across the bed that was not his. In that moment Casas spun, letting go of the belt, clawed fingers streaking hipward.

A fury of bone and muscle enveloped him, carrying him backwards, away from the bed.

Casas had the strength of a bull; even with his arms pinned flat at his sides and off balance he was one to reckon with. His staggering stride fetched the man on his back crashing into the wall, drove him against it again. The man gasped, his grip loosened; Casas wrenched himself free and spun away, again clawing for the gun at his hip — getting hold of it. A hard right to the jaw loosened his hold, drove him sideways, fighting to keep feet under him. Before he could get himself collected Maffitt was onto him, battering him, pounding him with punishing fists.

For hard-breathing moments they stood foot to foot, slugging, grunting, snarling. Casas ducked and, twisting, fetched up a knee, brutally ramming it at Maffitt's crotch. Maffitt, swaying back, only partially escaped; the knee, taking him higher, jerked his mouth open, doubling him.

Casas should have finished it then but he passed up the chance in a reach for his gun. It was clearing leather when Maffitt, catching up the wired-together chair, swept it forward in a frantic arc. It broke against Casas' head and shoulders, laying open a cheek, one snapped-off rung staying in Maffitt's grasp. As the big Mexican staggered Maffitt slashed him across the chest. Casas dropped.

But he was like a cat, scrambling onto his feet before Maffitt, still wheezing, could get near enough to whack him again. The gun was leveling now, naked and glinting. Flame tore out of it as Maffitt brought the rung down across Casas' wrist. The Mexican yelled. He let go of the gun trying to get to the door, right hand dangling as Maffitt came for him. Casas, trying to dodge, tripped on his long shanked big-rowelled spurs and fell heavily, his head slamming into a corner of the crate.

Maffitt stood there, clammy, still sawing for breath.

"Get yourself covered." Without turning he bent over, got a fistful of black hair, pulling the head forward. With the breath whistling out of his throat he let go of it. Casas wouldn't be troubling anybody any more.

Somebody was bound to have heard that shot. Maffitt rubbed damp palms against the cloth of his pants. "We better get whackin'."

Three days later they pulled into Round Creek, Maffitt wearing Casas' gun; Katherin, dirty and bedraggled, looking like hell in Rosa's black-and-red dress. They'd been chased a few miles but not too formidably.

That bunch, without Casas' driving will, hadn't looked to have much heart for it.

"By God," Maffitt said, "I'll be glad to shove my boots under a table. My gut don't feel no bigger'n a fiddle string!"

The girl's pinched face looked across at him irritably. "You think this town will take rocks for money?"

Maffitt's red-rimmed stare went over the black horse. "We're going to have money." He sent a glance toward the buildings, pulled up and got down. "I'll ride the black. About two miles to go." He eyed her impatiently. "Cuff some of that dust off and fix up your hair. You'll put up at the Henry House. You won't need any cash till we're ready to go."

"We better stay together —"

"We're doing this *my* way. Get into a room and stay there till you hear from me."

She was too beat to argue. She swapped horses with him and he swung onto Afligido. She said nothing more but it was obvious she was thinking.

It was about one-thirty when they came onto the main street. Just the way he wanted it, the town half asleep. He pushed a hand out toward a sign. "That's the place. You stay there."

"Won't they wonder . . ."

181

"Sure they'll wonder, but you'll get a room. No Texan ever turned away a woman yet. Just do like you're told." He grinned around at her bleakly. "Summer or winter nobody waggles a finger short of three o'clock. Get your room and stay in it. Put a chair under the knob and try to make yourself presentable. Sleep if you want. I'll pick you up for supper."

He pointed Afligido into a side street and left her.

He was tired, bone weary from their hours in the saddle. But he felt no particular pain except in his back, a little stiff where the muscles had been wrenched in his fight with the river. His leg was all right and even his pistol-torn cheek had scabbed over, practically healed, as was the black's scraped hip.

He reckoned he probably looked worse than Katherin, not having shaved since he'd got out of Naco. He wasn't about to, either. Beard and scab was the best protection he had; they might be hunting for a guy with a beard but not this far south and east it didn't seem like. He knew Round Creek pretty well, having holed up here once about three years ago.

That sun was wicked. A sight too warm for this time of year. No prospect of snow this far from the mountains and, like he'd reckoned, hardly anyone on the streets. Old Man Barr would never come this far. Neither would the Border Patrol — even if they were still hunting him, which he doubted.

Nobody around here was going to recognize the horse; probably wouldn't anyhow the way he looked right now, all scabbed up and his hair full of cockleburrs. He'd better see that no hostler got to messing around with him. Poorer the hide the better off they'd all be. Maffitt even considered temporarily laming him, deciding against this. Ganted up like he was Maffitt reckoned they'd get by. But there was a couple of things no man could have been expecting.

Turning up the lane to Oberhorn's Feed & Livery, sliding off in front of the cavernous old barn, Maffitt was pleased he'd never had any dealings with Oberhorn. No reason in the world why Oberhorn would connect him with the gent who'd left town on a borrowed horse three years back. No reason for the marshal to.

Maffitt was starting up the runway when he heard the office door screak. Oberhorn hadn't changed much, still had most of his lard and that same oily grin; still wearing that sun-greened stovepipe and that hunk of braided leather his watch was tied onto going across his pinto vest like a ferry cable.

He came up with his shoe-button eyes in their folds of fat slanching over Afligido and not missing a hair. He reached out a pudgy hand but Maffitt said, "I'll take care of — watch out! He don't much cotton to strangers."

Oberhorn peered at him fishily, then shrugged and sank wheezily onto a bench. "Take that last stall to the left an' shut the damn door."

A man with a hayfork limped in from the back just as Maffitt, having unsaddled, was rubbing the black horse down with a gunny sack. He went on with his work and when he was done let the big horse roll and get himself dirtied up again. He found a rope halter and, leading Afligido into the stall, ran the shank through a ring above the manger, pulling it short enough to keep the horse on its feet. The stablehand said, "Want I should git some hay?"

"Keep away from him," Maffitt said; and then something in the sound of that voice pulled his head around. But the light here was poor and the fellow was in the worst of it, putting away his pitchfork. Maffitt, paying no further mind to him, got whole oats from a bin, making two trips with a half gallon measure, climbing into the loft then to shake down some hay. He changed his mind after he got up there and was coming down the stationary ladder when some elusive memory he'd been trying to track down suddenly slipped into place, fetching his head around sharply.

The guy was still there, still watching, still waiting, half concealed in the shadows. Cold sweat broke across Maffitt's shoulders. He knew the man now; it was the fellow he'd shot in the leg at McQuirchee's, and there was a gun in his fist, the lifted barrel of it aimed at Maffitt's back. He could see the wicked whites of the man's gloating eyes.

"Small world," Maffitt sighed; and leaped from the ladder. The walls rocked with the blasts as the man jerked his trigger. Then Maffitt was onto him, carrying him down but not able to keep hold of him. The stable was in an uproar laced with the snorting squeals of kicking horses. Both men rolled. The man with the gun lunged erect, hoarsely swearing. The gun winked again. Oberhorn was shouting when Maffitt, palming Casas' pistol, squeezed off one shot. The fellow flopped around on the floor and grew still.

"My God!" Oberhorn said. "Was that son of a bitch crazy?"

Maffitt didn't say anything. Several men came running into the place, pulling up with their stares about equally divided between the man on the floor and the still smoking pistol that was in Maffitt's fist. Maffitt's look skewered around. The sag-cheeked liveryman sleeved his moist jowls. "Clear case of self defense . . . I can't think what come over that fool."

They were all looking at Maffitt now. He punched out the spent shell and shoved in a replacement, clicked the gun shut and dropped it back in Casas' holster. "You want I should git the marshal?" someone said.

"I . . . guess you better," Oberhorn muttered, watching Maffitt. Maffitt nodded. "A couple of you others," the liveryman said, "haul that outa here."

A crowd was collecting about the front of the place but there was nothing Maffitt could do to prevent this. The marshal — same whip-lean lantern-jawed man Maffitt remembered — came pushing through as the pair Oberhorn had growled at were picking up the corpse. They let go when they saw the badge packer. He came over, took a look, waved them on and hauled around to eye Maffitt, pretty obviously the center of attraction.

"Well, what's the story?"

Maffitt was a lot less calm than he looked. If he denied all knowledge of the man, attention would inevitably focus on Afligido — the last thing he wanted at this point. "Had a run-in with him at Pearce a couple weeks ago; feller was a case-keeper over there. Couldn't seem to keep up with himself," he said.

"You're claimin' he was crooked?"

"My saying so got him fired — I didn't follow him here if that's what you're chewing on."

"What name you usin'?"

"My own."

The marshal's mouth tightened.

"Dale Maffitt," Maffitt told him.

The eyes of the marshal went thoughtfully narrow. "I've heard of you, Maffitt." He left it there, waiting.

Oberhorn said, "He never started this trouble — it was Hunsinger, pullin' while this feller's back was turned, comin' down from the hay. Hell, I seen the whole thing! Self defense pure an' simple. Hunsinger got off four blue whistlers before this guy ever reached for his blow-pipe — I'll swear to that, Marshal."

The marshal flicked a peculiar look at him; it almost seemed like he was weighing something, then his glance swung back to Maffitt. Maffitt, too, had been considering the liveryman, but whatever he was thinking he kept to himself, concealing his interest behind inscrutable cheeks. "Might be a pretty good notion," the law man mentioned, "if you was to keep right on travelin', Maffitt."

"You orderin' me out?"

"You got any legitimate business here?"

"I got a wife," Maffitt said. "She's legitimate enough."

"You watch yourself." The marshal looked at him stonily. "You're a tramp, for my money. I'm going to tell you, flat out, the next trouble you get into I'm going to put you in clink, an' I don't care who had the right of it. I'm going to salt you away till I find someone huntin' you."

He swung on his heel and pushed out through the crowd which began to drift away. There was a cold wind blowing through Maffitt's thoughts as he listened to their departure. Be a bad day for him if this star packer ever got down to cases; he had no doubt the man would do as he said.

His mind came back to Oberhorn. He found the liveryman slyly watching him. The man lowered one eye in a wink, jerked his head. Maffitt followed him into the office. Oberhorn, reaching around, pushed the door shut, lowered his paunch to a swivel and parked his heels on the desk.

"Rest your saddle," he said, and stoked his cheek with a fresh cut of plug.

Maffitt stood against the wall.

"You want Hunsinger's job?" Oberhorn said finally.

It would give him an obvious reason for staying, staying long enough anyway to get the stake he was after. On the other hand Maffitt was reasonably sure this wasn't why he'd been called in here. "All right," he said, "I'll take it. Now say what's in your mind."

Oberhorn tongued the dryness of cracked lips. "Give you eight hundred for him."

Maffitt grinned, too. "Any more up your sleeve?"

This was calculated to give the man pause but Oberhorn said, "Got your bill of sale handy?"

The stillness thickened. The liveryman's enjoyment sat fatly on his cheeks. "I could do you a lot of good in this town."

"Get it off your chest."

"Well, that black come from Mexico. I didn't see much of you last time you was through here; Marshal didn't either but I expect I could stir up his memory."

"You son of a bitch," Maffitt said.

"Now, now . . . name callin' ain't goin' to oil up no gate hinge. I'm a businessman, Maffitt."

189

"What do you want?"

"That horse could put me —"

"He could get you killed, too."

Oberhorn, seeing the rage in Maffitt's stare, dropped feet to floor but the brash confidence in his look wasn't shaken. "You ain't in no position to talk about killin'. I'm not alone in this place. Mebbe you better cool off an' think this over. I'm offerin' you a trade."

They both knew Maffitt was over a barrel.

"I can listen to reason but I'm keeping the horse." Oberhorn's pea-sized eyes were almost hidden in their folds of unhealthy flesh. The pudgy hands remained folded across the bulge of greasy waistcoat. His wheezy breath shook a little. He said at last, "I'm listenin'."

The man's eyes showed rancor but he answered readily enough when Maffitt asked what he had in mind. "Race him, of course. Ain't that what you come here for? Run him at Snake Stomper. Town'll git onto that hide with just about everything that ain't nailed down. Hell, we kin own the place — we could give it away!"

"You'd run the horse under your name?"

The liveryman looked at him. "I don't guess either of us is fools." He rasped a hand across his chins. "What you had in mind's no good here; we don't hide the horse, we advertise the hell out of him."

"You tired of this place?"

Oberhorn chuckled. "I'll git someone to front for us. We got to make a big noise, we got to pile it on, see? You don't know this place. Talk about *pride!* Some of these moguls . . . But never mind that; I'll furnish the hide."

"Lap and tap?"

"You think this is Chi, mebbe? 'Course it'll be lap an' tap. I can put hands on the best lap-an'-tapper —"

"My wife'll do the riding."

Surprise made Oberhorn for a moment look ludicrous. His eyes turned mean. "Now you look here —"

"You heard me."

"But Christ, man! A woman . . ." He broke off. Very slowly a grin crept across his cracked lips. "Can she ride? — I mean *really?* What's she weigh? Done a lot of —"

"Never done this before in her life," Maffitt said, "but she knows the horse and the horse knows her. Right now she'll weigh maybe eight-five pounds."

The liveryman said dubiously, "Well . . . all right. I'll coach her."

"You'll keep away from her. Completely."

The man's cheeks puffed out, the beady

191

eyes slitting wickedly. He came onto his feet, white and shaking with anger. Maffitt said mildly, "The ride part of this is going to be plumb honest."

"We're givin' 'em twenty pounds!"

Maffitt just looked at him. After some of the bluster fell out of the man Maffitt said, quiet, "Clobber your friends all you want but don't cross me. Don't put nothing into this without I've given the nod to it. The first thing I'll need is a thousand dollars."

"What!" Oberhorn recoiled as though Maffitt had stuck a gun in his gut. All the color drained out of his face, rushed back into it. "You think, by God, I'm —"

"Just get me the cash, today, or the deal's off."

The liveryman swelled up like a carbuncle. "Why, you connivin' . . ." The breath clogged in his windpipe and he said, half strangled, "One word out of me —"

"You're not cuttin' your *own* throat," Maffitt smiled.

"I'll see you in hell first!"

"You'll get there. No need to push."

Oberhorn grabbed hold of his head as though to make sure it was still where he thought it was. His eyes bulged, his wattles shook. He stamped around like he was walking on snakes but Maffitt just grinned, more relaxed than he'd been in a half month of Sundays. The man was caught in his own greed. It wasn't a pretty sight but Maffitt knew then the way this would go. He wasn't mistaken.

Oberhorn sloshed into his chair with a gusty exhalation.

"All right, I'll get it," he said with a bitter and hating snarl.

"What's the lick of that hide — how far do you want to run him? Will he do a full quarter?"

"Expect he's done plenty of quarters," Maffitt nodded. "At Hermosillo one evenin' he went three for three wins one right after the other. I've run him a half full out with the girl up."

"The girl?"

"My wife," Maffitt said shortly.

"How's he break?"

"You don't need to worry about it."

"The Snake Stomper," Oberhorn said, "will hit his full lick in the second jump but they've got him too fat. His wind's gone — he's short. They pushed hell out of him once while he still had distemper. He likes 400 or less if he can git it. We'll ask a half mile an' settle on 440."

Maffitt shrugged. He didn't care what distance the horse had to run; he'd have put

Afligido up against Bug Hunter or that Illinois whirlwind, Barney Owens, if he'd had to; he wasn't worried about any horse they were like to run into.

"Suit yourself," he said. "You'll be doing the talkin'."

Oberhorn got up and wiped his palms on his pantslegs. "I'll be doin' some of it, all right, but I'll find someone else to get this thing rolling. Make yourself comfortable. I'm goin' to the bank."

Maffitt, after the liveryman stalked out of the place, spent an uneasy few minutes thinking over the possibilities, finally shrugging the dangers aside for the moment. Any town of this size could be filled with risks for him, but he had to get a stake and this had been the likeliest place he could think of. There was money in this burg and plenty of free spenders. This was horse and cattle country with any number of fair to large outfits inside comfortable riding and if the deal was worked right . . .

There was no good worrying about it now. He was in Oberhorn's hands and as long as the man . . . "Ahr, to hell with it!" he said, and started cleaning out stalls. They might have to run but the chances looked good that they might run with filled pockets.

He owed the girl that much.

14

Oberhorn, gone two hours, came back in a better — even expansive — frame of mind. Making sure they had the cavernous barn to themselves he tucked a fat rubber-banded roll of bills into Maffitt's pocket. "I've let drop a few words where they'll do the most good. Deal's set for tomorrow. Si Turner'll get things rollin' 'bout the middle of the mornin'."

"Turner?"

"Trey an' Deuce — biggest honkytonk in town." Oberhorn covered his chuckling teeth with a hand. "Si's got a heap to git even for when it comes to Snake Stomper an' Eli Grattison — a mighty heap."

There was nothing in the liveryman's words to alarm Maffitt; Oberhorn was already counting his loot, so pleased with the prospects he could write off that thousand like a keg of bad nails. Nor was Maffitt concerned to know more about Turner; somebody had to be cut in to get things started and it was obvious Oberhorn would pick his man with care; yet there was something . . .

"Who've you set up as owner?"

"Baboquiveri Stock an' Cattle —"

"You fool! That's a going concern!"

"Yep," Oberhorn smiled, "holdin's in Arizona. Wyomin' an' Man-yannerland. Nobody'll ask for *their* bill o' sale. Nobody'll question 'em sendin' a horse here for standin'. Hell, you couldn't find a better place than Round Creek to put a stud if a man's intention is t' git his colts around." He said with a visible satisfaction, "This deal is goin' to be pulled right. I'm havin' some cards printed advertisin' the horse at five hundred a season — another five if you want a foal guaranteed. By mornin' I'll have 'em all over this town."

"An' by noon this barn'll be swamped with gawpers. I don't like it."

"You can hole out up in the loft if you want."

"You goddam fool! That horse —"

Oberhorn chuckled. "I've let it be known he's bein' shipped in. We'll have to pick him up from the railroad. We'll hit out of here soon's it's dark."

"I'm not figuring to take root here."

"No need to. Turner'll fix up the race for

Sunday — day after tomorrer. You can head for the tules with Afligido just as quick after that as . . ." He quit talking, suddenly rigid, at the ominous look of Maffitt's face. "Now wait a minute —"

"That the name you told them to put on those handbills?"

The stableman went back a step, half throwing an arm up. But when Maffitt failed to come after him some of Oberhorn's confidence began to return. "Hell, nobody'll believe it — not really, I mean. They'll just figure it's another hide tradin' on a better nag's rep. We got to sucker Grattison into this — we got to paint up a picture that'll tickle his vanity."

"Paint!" Maffitt said. "You ain't got the sense to pound sand!"

Oberhorn, flushing, growled in tight-lipped defiance, "When this thing's over we'll be wadin' in it, both of us."

"Running a stallion that quick after shippin' — that quick in strange country! You ought to have your head looked at!"

The fat man grinned. "I been around a fortnight or two."

"And where'll you be when I take off with that horse? The horse you've claimed to be standing for service?"

Oberhorn, staring, put more distance between them. "This town knows me. Can I he'p it," he whined, "if some bum steals the horse?" He threw out an arm. "Now don't git your tonsils up. You'll hev enough dough t' git clean t' Argentina . . ."

"I hope," Maffitt said, "you know what you're doin'."

Oberhorn grinned thinly. "You'd better go put on the nose bag; we got a long ride ahead of us."

"Ride?" Maffitt looked at him blankly.

"You got to he'p me fetch this horse from the railroad. The suckers've got t' see Afligido git here — Sure, I know somebody mebbe's already seen him. I got that figured, too."

Round Creek was much as Maffitt recalled it, a little bigger, more saloons, a few more houses along the hill's upper crust. He saw Grattison's packing plant off in the distance. When he got opposite the Trey & Deuce he had a distrusting impulse to size up the fellow that would front for this job but better judgment prevailed. There was no point taking more chances than he had to. He'd have liked a fresher look at the race grounds too but strode on toward the Henry House studying the place again in his mind. It was a typical county fair layout as he recalled, plank seats and a bull ring — a half mile circle graded originally for trotters. He remembered the cattle pens, the leaky sheds for out-of-town horsemen. He hoped it would be *poco bueno* with Afligido; them Mexicans must have run him on just about everything.

He remembered snatches of the stories he had heard. Of how gaunted the horse had looked when he'd first seen him at Olivares' ranch, so thin he could have squeezed through the eye of a needle; and his feet — God Amighty! Those fellers who had raced him in Mexico had been made wealthy by him, yet would uncaringly walk him over cobbled streets for miles to the race track where they would then trot, gallop and jog him till his sweat disappeared, then unconcernedly walk him home over those same bone-jolting blazing miles. They'd never bother to cool him out, would most generally carelessly tie him to a tree and there let him stand through the heat of the day. At four in the evening when the heat got more bearable they would again pick up his rope and walk him over the hard streets till dark. He was fed at night on oats and an armful of cornstalks for roughage. "By the day of the race," one jasper had declared, "he was so damn poor you could count every rib — he

199

was practically dead on his feet. Yet with his owner's son up — weighin' a hundred and forty pounds — and a sear singer, he'd shame lightnin' by comparison."

Maffitt could only guess, but all the signs and signal smokes the horse stood to be at least twelve years old, maybe more. He didn't look it. You had to really know horses or see his teeth to give this any credence at all.

Someway, then, Maffitt got to thinking about the home place and about the outlander now enthroned there. Breeding wanted the horse, of course, for his blood and the speed he might put into whatever he got from Bridle Bit mares. No man with savvy would ever figure to run him at his age against the kind of horses currently in competition. Texas horses today, the best of them anyhow, were real speed merchants. Maybe a couple dozen men were turning out the kind of stock that could get any job done, be it cow work, polo or flatout racing; these cowponies were really taking over the polo field. But this wasn't Fort Worth or Alice or Denton; this was Round Creek, a town trying belatedly to get into the swim. Afligido ought to have one more race in him . . .

He got to wondering again what had happened to the Old Man and what part Cecil Breeding had played in what had caused the Old Man to do what he had done. In spite of all the evidence Maffitt just couldn't see his father drinking himself into a hole in the ground.

If there'd been anything underhanded it would be pretty hard to come up with now, just about impossible for a man in Maffitt's boots. Tracing back in his mind he couldn't be sure about anything. His tough luck on this venture was predicated on facts; it didn't necessarily follow that Breeding had helped to shape those facts or had had previous dealings or any conspiracy with Olivares. If anything, it was *circumstances* Breeding had conspired with to get Maffitt off back, the impact of circumstances on the reputed character of the man he'd sent with a thousand dollars to acquire a horse any fool would know would be held at a price considerably higher. The man had counted on Maffitt's bent for violence . . .

Well, Breeding had got rid of him. He couldn't go back there now. Time this was over he'd be lucky to get out of the country. He didn't trust that liveryman half as far as he could throw him.

He went back to the hotel. The Henry House lobby with its banjo clock and threadbare rug, its horsehair sofas and spur-scarred straightbacked chairs primly crescented back of the dusty rubber plant, looked about as he'd expected — even the faint smell of slippery elm, by which he reckoned the same nearsighted half-deaf clerk would still be passing out the keys.

And he was. Peering up over his spectacles he took in Maffitt's look. "Sorry," he said, not sorry at all. "We're full up."

"Good way to be." Reminded of his hungers Maffitt turned the book around and leaned over it. Picking up the pen he dipped it and scratched *Mr.* in front of the *Mrs.* where Katherin had signed. He wheeled away from the desk and climbed the stairs, not even sure in his own mind what he was up to. He could still see the girl as she'd looked with the top of her dress half torn off.

He found the door, softly knocked. "It's me — Maffitt," he said, and tried the knob. The door didn't give much. He guessed she'd taken his advice. He used his knuckles again, louder. He heard bed springs screak. Her muffled voice said, "Wait —" and he heard bare feet padding over the floor. "Who is it?" she said; and he said, "Maffitt. Open up."

There was a considerable silence. When

she pulled the chair away and he stepped in she had the black-and-red rag that had been Rosa's dress held up against the front of her. She thought he looked at her rather oddly, over-intent and over-long and, even though she still had her underthings on, heat came into her cheeks. She stepped back around the bed, a little unsure of him, afraid to breathe almost. After all they had been through this was ridiculous; but four walls made a difference.

She tried to keep these things off her face, to keep their relationship on that same impersonal level they had started with, but this was hard for her to do with that queerness playing through his stare. She had practically forced him to marry her; she didn't want to think of that now — didn't want *him* to. Things were all mixed up in her mind. So much had happened . . . so much had been shared . . . What if he insisted . . .

Her cheeks got hot, she grew pale about the mouth. Behind those unsightly scabs and whiskers she got the notion he was amused as he brought around a chair and straddled it. He folded his arms across its back. She wished with a tinge of mounting apprehension he would quit staring at her.

"Say something!" she cried; and now he grinned openly.

She clutched the dress tighter. The air in this room was hard to breathe. The walls were crowding her into a corner.

He put a hand in his pocket and brought out a roll of bills. Uneasy but fascinated she watched with thudding heart as he peeled off a couple and carelessly tossed them on the rumpled bed.

"Wh— what have you done?"

Maffitt, putting away the roll, grinned. "We're fixing to have a horse race. You'll be riding. Get yourself some pants an' a shirt. Better latch onto some glad rags, too. Get fixed up and put some grub under your belt and don't say nothin' about that horse."

He got up and stood looking across the bed at her, eyes like smoky sage in that light. She felt suddenly cold and bare and alone. Maffitt said testily, "I'll be gone for a while. I'll try and eat dinner with you tomorrow."

15

Back on the street Maffitt thought briefly of getting spruced up, decided against it. The less attention he attracted the better chance he might have when it came to shaking the dust of this place. He'd get a needle from Oberhorn and sew up his shirt, wash off some of the stink if he had time, maybe trim his beard a little. He suffered no pangs of conscience for what had happened to Hunsinger, nor did he feel at all guilty about this race they were promoting. He hadn't come here to keep cases on fools.

Oberhorn if he could would find some way to cross him, but that was to be expected. It was the skin-and-bones marshal he thought about mostly. That gent was strictly business; probably right now going through his dodgers trying to hook Maffitt up with something. Maffitt knew mighty well there'd be handbills, account of the girl and that fellow they'd left afoot in the desert, but he didn't think any dodgers had got this far yet.

He saw a couple of men pitching horseshoes out back of a hoof shaper's shop and felt mildly resentful that ordinary folks were still going about doing ordinary things. His thoughts touched Katherin again, considering the way she had watched him, the way she had looked on that bed when he'd jumped Casas. She'd been *glad* to see him then.

He scowled into a hash house and put away a meal, taking doubles on everything; one thing he didn't have to watch was his figure. The girl had been afraid of him. Yet back of Katherin's uneasiness . . . He said *To hell with it*, shoved up and paid his bill and took the shortest way to the livery. One of these times if he didn't keep a close hold he'd probably get the hell scratched out of him!

There was no one about when he went into the barn. The place was thick with shadows. He went over to where he'd left Afligido and made sure the horse was still in his stall. He went through to the back then, found a couple of hands emptying barrows on the manure pile. He saw them watching him from under their hats. "I'm the new man, Maffitt. Boss leave any orders?"

He could see they knew about Hunsinger. It was in their eyes, in the short way the bigger one finally grumbled, "Said you could give us a hand with this crap till he got back."

"All right. You lug and I'll shovel."

They were still at it when Oberhorn after dark came into the lantern light and beckoned. Maffitt went over and rinsed his hands in a trough and followed the liveryman into the office. "I got you a coat." Oberhorn held it out to him. "This is shaping up fine; there's talk goin' around a'ready." He considered Maffitt with his head to one side. "If you'd scrape off them whiskers an' let me git at that hair you could pass for a feller sent along with the horse. That way, when you clear out," he said persuasively, "there'd be no question of the nag bein' stole. I could shrug the whole thing off by sayin' you'd changed your mind, didn't cotton to the mares you'd seen around here."

Maffitt stared at him thoughtfully.

A handler of sufficient caliber to be sent by Baboquiveri with a horse important as the supposed Afligido might well be expected not only to be married but to fetch along his wife. It gave the whole setup a more authentic flavor. But the law —

207

anyways some parts of it — was hunting for that black and for the man last seen with him. Maffitt had to remember they were outlaws now, that there was more than dead men nosing at his tracks.

He said, "No" scowling, but the fat man sensed the hesitancy.

"Be a lot less chance of somethin' goin' wrong. Git the marshal off your back. Sure, you told him you was Maffitt, but that guy was a saddle bum. This way, reppin' for Baboquiveri, you could be the *real* Maffitt. Fixed up he'd never know you."

Maffitt eyed the fat man narrowly. He was about as smooth a talker as a man was like to run into.

"I want the same thing you want," Oberhorn growled. "I want t' git fixed an' I don't want no trouble. No matter what, that marshal's got a job to do. The guy that downed Hunsinger's goin' to git a mort of attention; best thing you can do is cut loose of him. You want to play this my way I'll stake you to the duds."

"Just changin' clothes and scraping off whiskers ain't —"

"I got more in mind than that. Fact is, I've already got the clothes, if you'll wear 'em — not bought here. Stuff I had when I come, that I'm too fat fer."

This was a hard man to know.

"I ain't goin' to argue," Oberhorn said. "Ain't my neck you're foolin' with; you wanta stick it out you go right ahead. Whiskers may look to you like a good cover but to the badgepackers they stick out like quills on a porkypine. Special if the badge is huntin' somethin' fishy."

Maffitt couldn't seem to make up his mind.

Despite all the liveryman's fuming and fretting it was near ten o'clock and darker than the inside of Jonah's whale before they got around to leaving. The yard hands were gone and the rheumy-eyed souse employed by Oberhorn as night man was comfortably settled in the office with a bottle when the fat man finally tipped Maffitt the nod. "You'll be ridin' the black; take care of this bundle. Don't lose the damn thing. It's goin' t' help put this over."

Able only to feel in these heavy shadows Maffitt judged the thing to be a folded blanket. Saddling up he tied it back of the cantle. "What am I supposed to come home on — Shank's mare?"

They'd slipped out the back way, circumspectly moving across vacant lots. They were clear of town before the liveryman spoke. "I got a horse staked out for you.

209

Everythin' we'll be needin' is waitin' up the trail a piece."

"Reckon you're bearing in mind what happened to Hunsinger."

Oberhorn's face came around, turned still. He relinquished a sigh, very smooth, not overdoing it. Presently he said, quiet and serious, "Chance like this comes just once in a lifetime. If that don't signify, nothin' I kin say will."

There was no more talk. There weren't many stars and the few Maffitt could see didn't shed enough light to guide even a hawk, but the fat man never cast around or appeared to hesitate. "About there," he said finally after they'd been riding a couple of hours. "Figured we'd better go far enough to make it look like we actually went over there; Butterick's Sidin's about another ten mile. Nothin' there but a tank an' cattle pens. Train'll be through around five in the mornin'. We'll be workin' most of the night."

The terrain became more roughly cut up. They did considerable twisting and turning, the ground dropping steeply under them now. By the sound they appeared to be threading a dry wash. Oberhorn was moving carefully. Maffitt heard a horse nicker, hollow sounding in this murk; both their horses answering. "All right," the liveryman said, stopping abruptly. Saddle leather creaked as he got down, the unseen horse blowing nervously. Maffitt sat stiffly still, intently listening, one hand on the butt of Casas' pistol.

A match exploded in the fat man's cupped palm, showing his bent-over shape crouched above a pile of sticks. The fire took hold, the orange blaze swiftly spreading, the heavy masses of shadow becoming great rocks in the flickering light. Maffitt saw the other horse, a bay gelding, picketed in bunch grass with enough rope to let him reach a pool of water fed by a green-scummed seep in the nearer gulch wall.

Oberhorn grinned. "Ain't nobody goin' to spot us here. Might's well git down an' rest your saddle." Going to his own he loosened the cinches, untied a bulky pack and tossed it down beside the fire. "You're goin' to have to he'p with this."

He got the pack opened up. There was a bottle and swabs, a currycomb, brushes, clean rags, clothes, a hat and a pair of Hyer boots, also an ornamented shell belt and holster with tie whangs. And a pistol.

There was nothing fat about Oberhorn's head. Maffitt, sharply eyeing him, got off Afligido and removed the folded-up blanket. He shook this out, curious, and found it to be what is known in trackside parlance as a "cooler," a horse blanket in the racing colors of Baboquiveri's stables, bearing the ranch's big sewn-on brand.

Coat off, Oberhorn was rolling up his sleeves. Observing the direction of Maffitt's testy glance he said, "You can put them duds on later." He picked up the bottle and a handful of swabs. "Better move him handy to that pool. You do the holdin', I'll do the work."

Maffitt loosened the cinches and led the horse over. Afligido, cocking pointed ears, rolled his eyes when the fat man started working with the swabs. He snorted a couple of times when the wet cotton came against him; then, soothed by Maffitt's voice, disposed himself in hipshot patience.

It was not a short process. It took a lot of water and a considerable amount of scrubbing. When Oberhorn finally stood back to look him over the big stallion had a star, a snif, a left white pastern and white up to the knees of both front legs. "There," the fat man said, standing back, "I guess that does it. An' it won't run off. He'll be like that till the hair grows out — looks natural enough don't it?"

Maffitt had to admit that it did. It considerably changed the stallion's appearance. Oberhorn said, "We'll leave the feet go. I'll take care of them after the town's looked him over. We better work on his tail now, thin it, shorten it, get him deburred an' curry him up some."

It was pretty near day by the time they finished. The black looked like a fast-mover now, like the pure-quill article he actually had been. Maffitt, breaking a long silence, said, "How'd you know this was Afligido?"

"Saw him about seven year ago — that time he beat Ridge Runner over in Chihuahua. Gawd, that was a go! Three lengths of daylight an' the kid never touched him."

"You figure he'll still run?"

Oberhorn showed his gold-filled teeth.

"They're going to know he's old when they look in that mouth."

The fat man snorted. "You don't think Grattison would ever be fool enough to run that hide of his at Afligido, do you? He's a real shorthorn, that guy! So he looks this nag over. Three white feet — I kin see the wheels goin' round in his head. He knows damn well it ain't Afligido, but the teeth are right. So he thinks we've been took in by the owner; he won't hev to be sold, he'll sell himself. He's a guy likes to crow; he'll pile every cent he's got on this go. An' there'll be a heap of others doin' the same."

He wiped his hands. "Now, what about you? You playin' this my way?"

Maffitt looked at the horse. He was convinced there was a wild card somewhere in this deal but his head was too filled with loose ends to find it now. If he was ever to put the past behind he needed the stake this race could secure for him; it was why he had come to Round Creek in the first place — getaway money. And the girl would be riding; she couldn't be tampered with. "I reckon," he grunted, but still not liking it. The trouble, he figured, if it came would be afterwards.

He went over to the blanket and picking up the pistol flipped open the cylinder. No loads in it. So there was no trick there. The barrel wasn't plugged. He snapped the trigger a couple of times. The action was okay.

Oberhorn snorted. "Peel off that shirt an' let me git at that hair." He picked up the bottle, held it up to the light, held it under the water till it was almost full again. Maffitt took off the torn shirt and the fat man got to work. "We don't want it lookin' like the horse; a kind of salt-an-pepper gray," he said, "ought to be about right for the part you're goin' to play." He worked a little across Maffitt's upper lip. When he was through he cut Maffitt's hair and handed him the razor and a bar of yellow soap.

Maffitt kicked off his pants and got it all over, blowing and splashing like a colt. When he dried off on some of the rags and got into the underwear and flare-bottomed pants Oberhorn, with his back against a rock and his legs stretched out toward the flaking coals of the fire, watching him pick up the razor, said, "Better leave a mustache. I'll cache these duds of yours under a rock; no use makin' a stink tryin' t' burn 'em."

He got gruntingly up after a while and rubbed the cramps out. "Goin' to take a look around," he said, and wheezed off up the gulch.

Maffitt finished up fast, mouth tight, narrowed eyes swinging around and about all the time. This was probably all right but if the man was going to try anything Maffitt meant to be ready for it. He got into the clean white soft-collared shirt, shrugged into the coat and strapped the gift cartridge belt about his lean middle. He filled the pistol's cylinder from the loops of Casas' belt, got the roll from his discarded pants, pushed his feet into fresh socks and stamped into the expensive boots. Everything fit like it had been made for him although none of it was actually new. The fat man had even provided him with a second-best stetson, gray like the pants and flat of crown, California fashion.

He picked up Casas' gun, finally sighed and, emptying the cartridges out of it, dropped them into a coat pocket. Then he pushed the pistol with the rest of his discarded stuff under a rock and scuffed some sand up against it. The liveryman wheezed into sight, looking Maffitt over with evident satisfaction. "Nobody'll connect you with the guy that gunned Hunsinger." He looked around, picked up his razor and soap. "I guess," he said, "we might's well git started. Better put that blanket on the horse; he's got to look right. Wants t' show a bit of lather when we git in. Gluck can cool him out while we eat."

"You think of everything, don't you?"

The fat man didn't bother answering that.

They had Afligido on a lead rope and rode the most of an hour without saying a word, Maffitt suddenly pulling up. Oberhorn, following the younger man's scowl, stiffened and swore.

Fresh tracks and plenty of them. Horse tracks coming from the direction of the railroad and heading toward town. The two men looked at each other, neither liking it.

"Could be a bad break," Oberhorn said, pushing it around in his mind. "Somebody bringin' in some stock, mebbe a race string. Six riders, ten head of loose horses."

"If they came off that train they'll damn well know *we* didn't."

The fat man was worried, no getting around it. "We could wait. Be another train tomorrer."

"And maybe another load getting off it. That's no damn good. We better play this like it lays."

"God damn it t' hell!"

"Kickin' your hound ain't going to help none. Be their word against ours. Maybe they're strangers. Could we have flagged the train down the line and got him off?"

"It's been done." Oberhorn scowled. "But what reason would we have?"

"Got a late start, saw we couldn't make it?"

The fat man shook his head. "He'd of been billed to that sidin'. If we'd took him off ahead of there those jaspers would've —"

"We'll stand pat," Maffitt said, "and keep our traps shut."

"Guess that's all we kin do. If the worse comes to worst —"

Maffitt's eyes were black. "We'll cross that bridge when we get to it."

16

Oberhorn didn't say much all the rest of the way in but it was apparent he was doing a considerable amount of thinking. It got into Maffitt's mind the man was holding something back; he looked jumpy as a cat.

This was a bad break, sure, but that bunch might not be going to Round Creek. Even if they showed about all they'd be able to say was that Afligido hadn't been on that train. What concerned Maffitt more was the size of the reception. Half the town, it looked like, was congregated on Oberhorn's premises.

"This Turner," Maffitt growled, "must have more tongue than a muley cow."

The liveryman managed a kind of sour smile. A chunky cigar-chewing dude in store clothes and brown buttoned shoes stepped up to run sharp eyes over the blanketed horse as the fat man and Maffitt swung down, Maffitt stiffly.

Turning Afligido over to one of his hands, Oberhorn told him to walk the horse around until the animal was sufficiently cooled to be put inside. "Si," he said, turning back to the cigar-chewer, "this here's Dale Maffitt from Baboquiveri. Maffitt, shake hands with Si Turner. Si'll bet on anythin' from jumpin' beans to a busted flush — an' mighty quick if the other guy's holdin' it."

Turner, grinning, closed a dry grip on Maffitt's hand. "Maffitt?" he said. "You the feller that snuffled that stablehand's light?"

Maffitt looked at him blankly. Some of those nearest began to stretch out their ears. Oberhorn, glancing under shaggy brows at Maffitt, said, "That *is* queer, now you come to mention it." To the man from Baboquiveri he said, "I got a saddle bum workin' here — turned out to be tolerable quick on the trigger — goes by the same handle you do. Killed a man yesterday." He watched Maffitt, weighing him. "This jigger told the marshal *his* name was Dale Maffitt."

"You say this guy works here?" Maffitt frowned. "Maybe I better have a look at him."

"Gluck —" Oberhorn called to the mousy hand walking the black, "tell that new feller t' come out here a minute."

219

"Boss, he ain't been around this mawnin'."

"Well, see if his nag's —"

"It ain't. I already looked."

Oberhorn shook his head, looking disgusted. "Kind of he'p you git nowadays . . . Marshal musta scairt 'im more 'n he let on." He stared around dubiously. "Claimed he had a wife in town, too."

"My wife's here," Maffitt said, "least, she's supposed to be. Come coupla days ago; wanted to stop by her mother's. Guess I better be —"

A man came shouldering through the crowd. There was a wink of metal. Maffitt suddenly stopped talking. The marshal said to Oberhorn, "That feller you had around here yesterday — where's he at?"

Oberhorn spat and shifted his chaw. "Give out his name was Maffitt — remember? This here's Dale Maffitt; just come in from Baboquiveri. Fetched in a horse I'm fixin' t' stand."

The lawman's pale stare went over Maffitt and swiveled back to skewer the liveryman. Oberhorn said, "Guess he took your advice. We was just talkin' about 'im. Gluck, there, says he ain't showed this morning. Somethin' on your mind, Marshal?"

"If that gazebo's who I figure he is they're

keepin' a cell warm over at Yuma for him. Grabbed a horse in Mexico, girl in Arizona. Left a border patrolman afoot someplace near Antelope Wells. Wanted for questionin' about it, anyhow. There's a two thousand dollar reward on that ranny!"

Maffitt stood there stiffly. Oberhorn's mouth fell open. Turner said, "A walking gold mine." The marshal glowered at the liveryman bitterly. "If you hadn't took up for him —"

"Nothin' else I coulda done." Oberhorn scowled. "Hunsinger got off four shots at the feller before this guy ever knew what was happenin'."

"Then, with just one shot, he chops Hunsinger down!"

"Well," Oberhorn said, a little gray around the jowls, "that's how it was."

"Didn't he claim," Si Turner put in, "he had a wife —"

"*My* wife," Maffitt said, "is at the Henry. I better —"

The marshal hardly glanced at him. "I looked into that — just come from there. Nothin' to it." He waited till Maffitt got out of earshot. "Real high class-fine looker. She never see that feller; alls she could do was shake her head."

Maffitt, having good ears and a high de-

221

gree of interest, caught that much and then bethought himself to ask one of the towns-men on the fringe of the crowd which way to the Henry House. The fellow took his arm and, at the edge of the street, pointed. "Right there."

"Obliged to you," Maffitt said, and struck off.

But there was no relief in him. That mar-shal's garrulity could be deliberate, de-signed to lull Maffitt into thinking he had nothing to fear. The man's eyes were sharp. The prowl of Maffitt's thoughts kept turn-ing up loose ends. He should have kept his mouth shut. Sure, that starbacker might have meant every word. He might likewise be thinking to give Maffitt all the rope he would take. *Rope . . .*

Sweat cracked through the pores of Maffitt's skin.

The guy they were hunting had run off with a girl, and that saddle bum yesterday had claimed to have a wife here. Maffitt, be-cause Katherin was registered in his name, had been forced just now to claim her — no matter that he'd aimed to. These were facts the marshal couldn't hardly miss. Could the man be fool enough . . . And there was that other time Maffitt had been here, not calling himself Maffitt but not bearded, either.

Three years ago. But he'd got out of this town on another man's horse.

And that slippery-elm chewing clerk! Near-sighted, wearing cheaters . . . Must have registered Katherin still clad in her rags; and he'd got a good look at Maffitt yesterday. These things might have thrown the marshal off, convincing him the killer had hooked himself up with a spurious identity simply because there was, as it happened, a woman of that name on the hotel's books.

But the girl had come with no baggage. She might have thought to account for her appearance, to claim her bags were held up or checked somewhere — she was smart enough to have done this. She might have bought bags when she bought the clothes with the money Maffitt had given her . . . But it was a fact she'd come without bags. It was a fact Dale Maffitt, from Baboquiveri, had also showed up without luggage. Two more things for the marshal to chew on. And this new Maffitt had admittedly come in with a horse that was very much in the news. Or about to be.

Supposing the marshal wired Baboquiveri!

Maffitt's throat was dry. He stepped into a saloon and downed two shots of best bottle bourbon, produced his roll and peeled off the smallest bill he could find, a fifty. The place happened at the moment to be without other patronage, but the barkeep looked at the bill and shook his head. "Ain't you got no loose change?"

Maffitt mentally winced. A few more of these blunders . . . Before this caught up with him might be out of that marshal's reach. He might be beyond caring.

The barkeep pushed back the bill, grinning feebly. "Compliments of the house," he said; and Maffitt got out of there.

He wanted to take off the coat and before he'd walked much farther he did, stepping into the hotel with it over his arm. The same bespectacled clerk was back of the desk but before Maffitt managed to get tangled in talk with him, he saw Katherin sitting on a sofa and went over. She was wearing her new stuff.

She looked up, puzzled by his approach. He had his hat in his hand. Her eyes got big; all her color fled suddenly. She came to her feet. Maffitt grabbed her and kissed her — a bit too emphatically, perhaps for a husband, but it effectually silenced her and that was the main thing. "We better eat," he muttered, letting her step back.

Her eyes were still big but she took his arm and, without appearing to do so, guided him across the dim lobby and through a narrow arch into a big room filled with tables. No one else was eating but Maffitt pulled out chairs against a wall and they sat down. A waitress poked her head out of the kitchen. "Be a half hour yet —"

"We'll wait," Maffitt told her and, when she disappeared, he dragged a hand across his forehead.

Katherin leaned forward. "This is wonderful! No one would ever guess —"

"You look pretty good yourself," he growled, "but we better get down to brass tacks." He brought her up to date on his activities, not forgetting the horsemen who'd come into town ahead of them or his suspicions about the marshal.

"I think you're being oversensitive," she said. "He talked with me. I don't think he suspects a thing. He knew that tramp had skipped before he saw you at Oberhorn's stable; he's been combing the town. He told me himself he reckoned the fellow had dug for the tules. And those people you mentioned who came in with the horses, they're camped at the fairgrounds. Everybody knows about them — some big outfit that's got a race booked with Snake Stomper. It's the talk around town —"

"What'd you hear about Afli?"

"They're talking about that, too. Nobody thinks he's got a chance — there's talk of making a three-horse race of it, running the whole thing off at one lick."

Maffitt frowned. "You hear what the name of this outfit's —"

"Buck . . . Bird Chaser. Something like that."

Maffitt wasn't half listening, his thoughts already fastened onto something else. With the handle of his fork he was indenting nervous doodles into the coffee stained cloth about the rim of his turned-down plate. "Clerk's the one with the fire in his fingers. Must've thought it damn odd."

"I told him the Pecos stage had got wrecked, that I'd come in an ambulance with a patrol from Fort Stockton as far as Branton. I said I'd picked up a ride with a nester and his kids from there." She smiled at the memory. "He believed me, I think — he tried hard enough. I said my stuff was scattered all over ten acres, probably blown halfway to Corpus by now. When my husband —"

"Yeah," Maffitt said. "He'll sure as hell remember me!"

"I don't think so. He don't see very well. He told the marshal 'that range bum' took a look at the register and 'clumb the stairs' without opening his mouth. I said you must have gone somewheres else, no one had come to my door. I had on these clothes. He seemed a little in awe of me." She looked at Maffitt, amused. "He's going to be pretty shocked when I get into those pants."

Pretty indignant, too, Maffitt thought, or damned suspicious. They'd have to get out of this place like the heel flies was after them, and plumb lucky if they made it.

Maffitt was mightily tempted to give this deal up. Whether he'd swallowed their stories or not, John Law, after that ride, was going to be seeing a whole lot of things different. Trouble was, Maffitt was into this now. Oberhorn, if they left him the horse, would probably keep his mouth shut, but that damned marshal . . .

The waitress, smiling brightly at Maffitt, came over and took their order. Katherin's eyes took this in; her mouth got more in-tucked round the corners. Maffitt was too engrossed in his problems to notice any part of this. When the girl went away he said, "I hope you're smart enough to handle that horse. Whatever way it goes there'll be some jockeyin' for position. They'll try to get you flustered and catch the horse off stride. They'll try every dirty trick they can think of. If there was anyone else I could —"

"I can handle him," Katherin said confidently. "I've seen plenty of matched races."

"Main thing is, once you're clear, give the horse his head. He'll know what he's doin'. He's run all his life."

"This will be lap and tap, I suppose."

Maffitt shrugged. "No tellin'. It'll probably be whatever way this Snake Stomper bunch figure they've got the best chance at. Oberhorn will agree to anything. He's higher'n a kite on this horse; he's been counting his winnings ever since he laid eyes on him." He said thoughtfully, "He's pretty sharp. Anyhow, don't worry about gettin' Afligido off in front. Make sure he *gets* off, then give him his head."

Katherin nodded. "They've got it set for tomorrow evening. Four o'clock. A straight-out dash."

Maffitt looked at her sharply. "On that bull ring? It's a half mile circle."

"They've got a straightaway too. Scraped it last year for the match between Snake Stomper and some horse called Honeysucker. The Snake won hands down. It was a 330 go. They couldn't even find the other horse for dust."

"I hope," Maffitt said, "they don't find us, either."

He looked pretty grim.

228

He spent the rest of the day around town talking down the idea that there would be any race. Oberhorn, furious, caught up with him in Turner's. "What do you mean there won't be no race!"

"I don't think," Maffitt said, eyeing the fat man distastefully, "the owners would take kindly to the idea of Afligido being put to such a risk. He hasn't been doing any running; they've retired him to stud."

The liveryman looked as though he were about to burst his surcingle. Si Turner's mouth thinned. One of the scowling townsmen growled, "They don't hev to know about it, do they?"

"You figure you could keep a thing like this quiet?" Maffitt looked around scornfully. The big room was packed and it grew suddenly still in a way that was ugly. It made Maffitt's hair crawl but none of his perturbation showed. He said derisively, "All who believe that can go stand on their heads."

There were snarls and growls from glowering faces. They were like a pack of cur dogs showing their teeth at the prospect of having a bone snatched away from them. Maffitt, a little uncertainly, backed off a step, one hand out behind as though reaching for a door. Their hostility became more pronounced, brightened now by a gleam of rising confidence. This interloper was finding he'd bit off more than he could chew. Pete Burgoo, the town barber, cried, "They won't know, by Gawd, till it's over an' done with!"

Turner's cold-jawed look caught Maffitt's eye, hauling Maffitt after him into his backroom office. Turner shoved the door shut. "You serious?"

Maffitt hesitated, swallowed uncomfortably. "I've got my job to think about. If I let the horse go into this and he gets took I'm liable to find myself walkin' down the road."

Turner took a wallet from the inside of his coat, stood tapping it against his other hand. Finally, flipping it open, he thumbed out a slim sheaf of bills, dropping them onto his desk in front of Maffitt. "I think," he said coldly, "we understand each other."

Maffitt, fanning the edges of the bribe, tucked the bills into his pocket. "I guess we do," he said, laughing shakily.

Turner opened the door, shooing Maffitt ahead of him. Every avid eye in the place was focused on them. Turner said, grinning thinly, "It's goin' to be run, boys. Drinks on the house."

They all knew Maffitt had been bought.

17

The drinks were downed, backs were slapped with a real Christian spirit, everyone's tongue going and nobody hearing a quarter of what was said. The crowd was feeling friendly and mellow in the glow of easy dollars as they individually sized up the angles and found the prospects truly salubrious. Saturday night and free drinks all around! Maffitt, so briefly the focus of indignant stares, was forgotten, no longer important now the race would be run. Five or six of the gabbier customers left to spread the glad tidings. Bets were offered, taken and posted, Snake Stomper odds-on at ten to one.

Back at the livery in Oberhorn's office the fat man dug up a cherished bottle and, wiping the dust off, pressed it, grinning. "Missed your callin'. They'll be diggin' up dough ain't seen the light in ten year! You had me sweatin', I'm frank to admit, but we'll put it over now. We'll quit this county the way Steel Dust left —"

"I hear," Maffitt cut in, "there's talk of making this a three-horse go." Actually the only mention of such a thing had come from Katherin, which seemed rather odd now he'd time to put his mind to it. But Oberhorn's sharp glance was confirmation. "Ol' Bug Hunter," the fat man nodded.

Maffitt's face tightened. "Mean to say these Snake Stompers'd let a horse like that in? He's got a record —"

"Been lamed since then." Oberhorn's eyes skittered away from Maffitt's. "Hell, that's howcome this bunch happen t' hev him. Some Arizona outfit — they admit they got him cheap. Anyways, they already had a run matched with Snake Stomper — bought the Bug unseeen, figurin' he was sound. They been tryin' t' crawl out but they had five thousand up; Grattison — that's Snake Stomper's papa — says they'll run or forfeit. Nothin' t' be scairt about," Oberhorn chuckled. "That's an old horse —"

"Afligido's no spring chicken!" Maffitt snarled, getting out of his chair. "This thing was risky enough the way it was in the first place. With Bug Hunter in it anything can happen. A third horse . . . You ought to be bored for the simples!"

In their pockets of flesh the fat man's eyes

glittered but he had a good hold on himself. All he said was, "We challenged Grattison; if Grattison wants t' ring Bug Hunter in I don't see that we've much ground for complaint. I seen the horse limpin' around myself."

Maffitt said harshly, "You fool enough to think this Snake can beat a record holder. It's for the *quarter* that damned horse holds his —"

"Might be there's a fix," Oberhorn said mildly. "I've seen 'em all run — saw the Bug make that record. If he's got troubles your black will make him look like a cart horse. An' so far as Snake Stomper goes, that's Grattison's worry; some guys'll take any kind of chance to lower or show up another bird's record."

"We ain't talking about birds," Maffitt said, eyeing him sourly.

Oberhorn, winking, suggestively chuckled. "I'm no fool," he said smugly.

Maffitt tramped around the cubbyhole with both hands shoved into his pockets, even more disturbed than he looked. The way this shaped up to him Grattison would back the Snake but only enough to prod up the suckers; his folding dough would be farmed out on Bug Hunter, along with everything he could beg, steal or borrow.

There didn't have to be any fix, but he couldn't get it out of his head that there was one. Bug Hunter, lame or sound, was worry enough for any galoot who'd got beyond playing with a string of spools. He'd won his record fair and square so far as was known, and in time that was really traveling — twenty-one seconds flat. Maffitt was one to respect ability but it was Oberhorn's ability that was making his skin itch. Maffitt couldn't shake the feeling the man was hiding something.

Yet he couldn't figure what the hell it could be. If it was something disastrous about Afligido the liveryman wouldn't be putting up dough. Which he was: he's left twenty-five hundred with the barkeeps at Turners. A pretty fair slug for these times and parts, and every thin dime of it on the black's nose. If it was the marshal . . . but Maffitt couldn't see himself free if the badge had anything solid to go on.

He guessed Katherin was right. He was jumping at shadows.

"How much did Turner give you?" the liveryman asked.

"If you're figgerin' t' hatch it . . ." Oberhorn said with his eyes like marbles, "Ain't bet a nickel yet, hev you?"

So here, Maffitt thought, was what had

got Oberhorn's george up. "Expect you're right," he said, grinning. "I'll get right at it."

Oberhorn, goosily eyeing him, bent to open the crackerbox he used for a safe. He got out a couple of folded papers — deeds, by the print on the front of them. "I'll go with you," he said, getting up. He put the papers in his pocket.

They made a round of the dives. Every one of them was packed. Cowhands in from roundabout ranches. Teamsters. Section hands. Bums. Cattlemen. Horsemen. Even a sprinkling of soldiers ridden over from the fort. Smart money now was leaning heavily toward Bug Hunter. The Snake was getting a good share of the play but the best Maffitt and Oberhorn were able to get was seven for each of their dollars invested.

Maffitt put twelve hundred on Afligido and the livery man put up his stable and a roominghouse. He showed no intentions of going home and when Maffitt, at two in the morning, suggested they'd better be getting back, Oberhorn said: "I've got three guys with shotguns lookin' after that hide and I'm stickin' right with you till you've got every cent of that dough put up."

"I've got a wife —"

"You never left it with her. I kin see the

bulge of it right there in your pocket."

"Thinkin' I might look up Bug Hunter's papa —"

"His boys has been around. They been coverin' their nag." He stared at Maffitt suspiciously.

"I was thinking," Maffitt said, "about them tracks we saw this morning. If that crowd made 'em how come they're keepin' their mouths shut: If we was standin' in their shoes —"

Oberhorn said, "They've got it doped out the black ain't Afligido. Couple of 'em come around while you was off with that piece of fluff —"

"You referring to Mrs. Maffitt?"

Oberhorn backed off a little. "All right. Mrs. Maffitt. They — these fellers — looked him over pretty good," he said sourly.

"You see the Bug?"

The fat man nodded. "No ringer there. Ain't limpin' now neither. Mebbe it's worse when he gits warmed up. Let's spend that money."

Maffitt was broke again, stony, when they crawled up into the loft. Three men sat around in the deep gloom below them, armed to the gills. Every lantern had been removed from the barn. Two hands with rifles patrolled the night outside.

★ ★ ★

It was six before Maffitt, still tired, got up. He'd have slept the clock around if Oberhorn had let him. "I'm eatin' with you," the fat man said. "I want a word with your wife."

They brushed the hay off their clothes and got down. The day crew had come and were working around. Three hard looking characters with cigarettes on their lips held down the bench outside the big doors. Oberhorn, paying off the night guards, passed their armament over to these boys. "Remember," he warned them "nobody — an' I mean *nobody* — gets near that horse. Keep everybody outa here. My hands'll stay out; they've had their orders."

Maffitt, glumly filled with his notions, tagged after the liveryman. The hard fate which had never let go of him was still conspiring with circumstances to force on him a responsibility he bitterly resented. His every instinct and experience urged him to cut and run, to get out from under before the past and this nightmarish present backed him into a corner there'd be no getting out of.

He reminded himself he owed her nothing but he was caught in a web that was stronger than steel, bound in his confusion by a tangle of things he could find no adequate excuse for. The girl had him hamstrung; she'd crept into the very blood and bone of him, by some magic of nearness coloring all his thinking to where he could no longer recognize even his own desires.

When Oberhorn, grunting under his burden of flesh, dropped onto the bench his new guards had just quit, Maffitt sat down gingerly, finally saying testily, "If you're fixing to do anything about his feet you better get at it. She won't be up yet and he ought to be getting used to the weight. You puttin' racing plates on him?"

"Polo plates," Oberhorn groaned, pushing up with a wheeze. "No rest for the weary. That's a damn smart horse. You notice he didn't clean up last night? Left half his hay, hardly touched his water. He knows what's comin'. Gittin' hisse'f ready. Ain't one in ten humans got that much savvy."

He pulled out his watch. "You don't need to worry none about that track. They've drug every inch of it. Drug it twice yesterday, wet it down last night. They'll keep at it all day." He disappeared inside the barn and Maffitt, still scowling, still fighting his phantoms, got up and went after him.

The fat man built up the fire in the forge while Maffitt haltered Afligido and backed

the big black out onto the runway. Oberhorn spoke again to the guards and picked
up his tools and got to work.

A man didn't need a fire to put on racing
plates. You could bend them with your
hands, shape them cold on an anvil; but
these plates were heavier. Maffitt said disgustedly, "Why don't you hitch that safe of
yours onto him?"

"They ain't softened that track as no favor
to us. This horse has got to be able t' git hold
of it. He's a hard-breakin' son of a bitch an' I
don't want t' find him down in no mud." He
stared up at Maffitt, filled with annoyance.
"Be trouble out there. It's no damn place for
a woman."

He got the worn shoes off, so thin in some
places you could almost see through them.
"Mex'kin!" he growled, scornful. He eyed
the black critically as Maffitt moved the
horse around. He got down on all fours,
clucking under his breath, and squatted a
while on his heels, darkly thinking. He
trimmed the black's hoofs, cleaned out the
frogs, prodding and poking, still muttering
under his breath. The shoes fitted, he
picked up each foot, almost appearing to be
weighing them by hand. He went back to the
rasp.

He spent two and a half hours at it then

got up, groaning, grunting. He went and washed his hands and arms in a trough while Maffitt put Afligido back in his stall. Maffitt dumped a gallon of whole oats in the feed box and cleaned every wisp of hay out of his reach.

At eight-thirty they stepped into the Henry House. Maffitt sent the night clerk to find out if Mrs. Maffitt would be dressed in time to eat with them. The man said she would, that she would be right down directly.

She took three-quarters of an hour. Oberhorn's jaw dropped when he saw her. He peered at Maffitt and back again and shut his mouth with a loud click of teeth. Then they all trouped into the dining room where, by this time, there were others eating. Every head wheeled to fetch the girl into focus. Oberhorn wasn't the only man impressed.

When their orders were given he leaned forward, very serious. "Sure you kin ride that black devil, ma'am?"

Katherin smiled. "I think so. He's gentle enough —"

"Ain't no studhorse gentle when he gits in a race. They got to hev edge, got t' be screwed up t' run. Uh . . . meanin' no disrespeck, ma'am, I'd feel a heap easier 'f I

240

could put a boy up."

"She'll ride," Maffitt said, and dug into his food. Katherin hardly touched hers. She drank three cups of black coffee.

When Maffitt pushed back, the fat man excused himself and stepped off to stoke his jaw. Wiping his mouth, reseating himself, he got down to brass tacks. "You'll know how t' ride the horse better'n I could tell you; I'm leavin' that part of it up t' your judgment. But there's a couple of things you better git straight. This ain't no parlor social. That pair'll be out t' win, no holds barred! There ain't a dirty trick in the book they won't try if it looks like you got any chance of beatin' 'em."

"I understand," Katherin nodded.

Maffitt said, seeing Oberhorn's skepticism, "She'll do what she has to do." The partisan confidence in her husband's tone fetched a sudden brightness into Katherin's glance. Oberhorn, studying the pair of them, grunted. "All right." He eyed Katherin grimly. "You ever rode in a race before?"

She shook her head. "But I know what it's like."

Oberhorn sniffed. "In a short go like this, most times anyway, gittin' off first is half the battle. But never mind that — ain't a chance you could do it. You'll hev t' come from be-hind. Don't let 'em fluster you. Both them jocks'll try t' make you see red; they'll try t' git your horse fouled up one way or another. Keep your head. Alls I want you t' do at the start is keep him from gittin' hurt — under-stand?"

"I think so."

The fat man, sighing, picked up his hard hat. "You better stay at the barn with us. Fetch whatever you'll need. We'll wait at the desk."

Maffitt, after she'd gone, got a cigar and fired up. He couldn't just stand there. They went back through the arch and found seats in the dim lobby but Oberhorn, unable to contain himself, heaved his bulk off the sofa and stomped around, taking out and re-placing his time-piece impatiently. "Might he'p our chances was she t' circulate around in that getup, but we jest can't risk it. I hope t' Christ," he growled, eyeing Maffitt, "you know what you're doin'!"

Back at the stable Maffitt walked Afligido in short stretches to limber the horse up. Two or three times they went all over him, rubbing him down, examining him criti-cally. Oberhorn, especially, kept feeling of his legs. Katherin tried to nap in a stall but the heat brought her out again.

At three o'clock Maffitt sponged Afligido's nostrils with a damp cloth and let the black rinse his mouth out. You could tell by the roll of his eyes the horse was high. All through the day there'd been a collection of lookers lounging and arguing beyond the guards out by the road. It was a wearing day. And that sun was like a big tub of fire.

Maffitt now took Afligido out and walked him some more, then left him tied to a leafless tree, thinking to simulate well as he could the conditions under which the black had raced for his Mexican owners. It might have seemed more practical to have taken him over the track but he was afraid of this and so was the fat man. The grounds would be packed by this time. Oberhorn, coming out of the barn, mopped his jowls and peered again at his watch. "Mebbe we ought t' be gittin' him over there." He eyed the horse anxiously. "Reckon he's ready?"

Maffitt said dryly, "I can't get a word out of him."

Oberhorn swiveled an irritable glance. "Git into your ridin' rig," he snapped out at Katherin, and called up one of his stable hands. "Git that blanket on him!" He glared at Maffitt, seemed to want to say more but, clamping down on the impulse, swung and waved in his guards.

"Want you boys t' stick right with us; I've put each of you on the black for a ten spot. Go fetch your horses." He said in Maffitt's direction, "I figure t' —" and stopped with his mouth open.

Katherin was coming from the barn in pants, red hair tied back with a blue scarf. The eyes of the guards stuck out like bugs on a stick.

"Just my wife," Maffitt said, and the fat man waved them onto the road. He came around personally to help Katherin into the surrey one of the hostlers led up, wheezed around and, tilting the vehicle precariously, heaved himself aboard to apprehensive sounds from the squeezed-flat springs. Picking up the reins he waved the whip and Maffitt, flanked by a brace of gun guards, led off.

18

No untoward incident marred their trip to the Fair Grounds; the trouble came after they got there. Maffitt knew it was trouble the moment he saw the man.

The whole town had moved out here and all the outlying ranches had managed to have at least one rep from their outfits, several of these crews obviously being in full roster. There were rigs of all kinds in all conditions of repair, from sodbusters' Red River carts to the fringed and resplendent yellow-wheeled vehicle from Madam Bisquanie's Palace of Joy filled with giggling pulchritude.

Ahorseback and afoot this multitude had gathered from the four ends of nowhere offering prodigious testimony to the efficacy of rumor. The warped and groaning grandstand looked in imminent peril of collapse. Popped corn and peanut venders plied their wares practically unheard in that huge and fluttery cacophony of voices; cowhands afork their tail-switching ponies made blotches of shifting color. Kids trying out their mustangs and puddinfoots went squealing and squawking around the bull-ring. The stockpen timbers were black with shapes.

All Maffitt had room for in his head right then was the big walloper — muscles straining every bind of his shirt — using shoulders and elbows to get through the arguing oglers grouped in a shifting clot between himself and this pen where the sprinters were readying.

Maffitt reckoned he knew now what had so upset Oberhorn. All along the fat livery-man must have known or strongly suspected what outfit had been on that train supposed to have fetched here the black Afligido. The big guy was boring straight and head-on for Maffitt, pulling a lot of hard looks along after him.

Maffitt let go the black's bridle as Ober-horn and Katherin, unable for the crowd to bring their surrey any nearer, were climbing down. It was apparent to Maffitt any help he got would have to come from himself. "Well?" he said, and Vechel Harris grinned.

"Looks like you kinda got lost with that horse."

Maffitt ignored all the signs he hung out and Breeding's Bridle Bit foreman, stopping just out of reach, said, "You want that bunch of flappin' ears in on this?"

"Have the boys get him ready," Maffitt called out to Oberhorn; "I'll be with you directly." Stiff cheeked he followed Harris off to one side, disregarding the stares and wheeling looks of those around them. "Make it short."

"That horse was supposed to be fetched to the ranch —"

"The deal," Maffitt said, "was that Breeding would pay three grand for Afligido. Nothing was said about me havin' to take it."

"You took that thousand bucks earnest money an' give a receipt." Harris grinned with his eyes two shades colder than ice. "Calls for a black named Afligido. It don't call for you to run him."

"You looked at this horse?"

"I know all about that ride he didn't take; I could hatch up a statement about what happened in that gulch." Chuckling he slipped a hand inside his shirt, giving Maffitt a look at Casas' pistol. Breeding's foreman was hugely enjoying this. "Next time you put somethin' under a rock —"

"You taking the horse?"

"You know better'n that." Harris' lips stretched out behind their bristle of hair. "I wouldn't want to deprive all these sports —"

"All right," Maffitt said, "I'm listening."

"Without you're huntin' a talk with that tinbadge you better pay real good attention."

There was plenty of room around them now, the bulk of those nearest having tagged along after the unheard-of sight of a female in pants and the white-stockinged black supposed to be Afligido. "I'm listening," Maffitt repeated.

Harris said, " 'Gido runs, does his damndest. But he's a old horse, bucko, an' don't you fergit it."

Buttoning the gun back into his shirt he stepped back.

Maffitt said, "What if Snake Stomper wins?"

Harris grinned. "The Old Man's got a lot of confidence in you. Ain't every walloper could git away with what you have. You can have the horse an' the dough you signed for; just be sure your rider understands how things are. Otherwise —" Harris' eyes were like knifeblades — "somebody might happen to fergit she was a woman."

With a final hard chuckle he wheeled about and walked off.

Maffitt knew when he was whipped. Nothing in this world was going to get him out of this one. He hadn't figured on Breeding or the possibility of Bridle Bit showing up at this place. He'd forgotten all about that money — the fool thing he'd done signing for it. Harris wasn't kidding. The black would lose or there was going to be more damn hell turned loose . . . And what about Katherin, plumb in the middle of it?

He looked over at the pen where they were saddling the horses. The crowd was still thick. He didn't see Breeding's ramrod. He couldn't locate the marshal, but there was no lack of horses. Nothing to stop him piling aboard one.

He tongued dry lips and wiped the back of his neck. Jamming through to the gate with his elbows he got into the saddling pen. Snake Stomper and Breeding's horse were already heading for the track, jocks up. Oberhorn, sweating, had hold of Afligido who was throwing his head and sidling around, blowing like he'd got rollers in his nose. Katherin, flushed, stood back of the fat man, ignoring the bold eyes and lewd grins, the sly nudgings. Maffitt's voice quieted the black. Oberhorn's jowls shook like turkey wattles. "Where the hell you been!"

His pale little eyes were ugly with suspicion.

Maffitt chewed on his lip, gave Katherin a leg up and handed her the reins. He tried the cinch and tugged it tighter. He shortened the stirrups. The fat man snarled, "They got a fifty foot score! Made it ask-an-answer!"

Maffitt looked at Katherin. "Just remember we're in this to win," he said grimly. "Don't let them get you rattled."

Up in the judges' stand a man with a megaphone was going over the conditions. *One feller will ask if the others is ready when they come up to the line. If both answers 'yes' he'll yell 'go!' and they will; but if one of them says 'no' the whole push'll turn back. They'll keep right on scoring till both answers agrees.*

"Damn fools!" Oberhorn growled. Maffitt said tightly, "Get hold of his cheekstrap and get her out there."

The fat man grabbed a handful of leather but, still in his tracks, leaned across his arm. "If this is a doublecross you've fixed up —"

"Get her out there!" Maffitt snarled, cocking a fist, and Oberhorn, still glowering, swung away with the horse. The megaphone roared: . . . *is probably the first time in history a three-horse go was ever turned loose by ask-and-answer. That's a match-race system but we're using her anyhow, like the*

Baboquiveris is ridin' a fe-male jock. . . .
Maybe there is something new under the sun.
Match-race style the jocks asks and answers but
in the interest of fair play the owners or reps for
same will do it . . . Owners or reps kindly go to
the starting line. You'll draw lots for first
ask . . .

Maffitt, mouth tight, headed for the track.

They had a straightaway, six hundred and sixty years long coming out of the bullring, which they'd closed off with a couple of saw-horses. It was sixty feet wide and seemed pretty well packed, down the center anyway. The sides Maffitt didn't much like the looks of; he saw spots where he reckoned too much water had stood, soft places where it had puddled and any horse forced into one of those . . .

There were four or five fellows where they'd gypsumed a starting line and it was plain, as Maffitt came nearer, that two of these were the marshal and Harris. If he could only find Breeding . . . but there was no chance now to look for him. The marshal's cold eyes slewed around and met Maffitt's, and someway Maffitt's glance was drawn to the man who stood by him, a stout, oldish gaffer with a mustache that curled round his jowls like rams' horns and watery green eyes that couldn't seem to stay still.

He had on a box coat with a green velvet collar turned up round his neck and both hands in its pockets as though they were wedged there.

The marshal said, "This here's the Baboquiveri rep, Maffitt," and, to Maffitt, "Grattison —" waving a hand at a beefy redfaced shape in blue store serge, "the Bridle Bit rep," nodding at Harris, "and Sheriff Barr who's come over here from Bisbee on a matter of business."

Maffitt's face felt stiff as caliche but he managed to pass out the nods all around though the breath was too stuck in his throat for him to say much. Even when the marshal declared Barr one of the judges Maffitt just stood there like he didn't hear well. Grattison's nod was perfunctory. Harris muttered something and Katherin's father, staring off toward the finish, never opened his mouth.

Now the marshal was pushing a fistful of matches at them. "Shortest asks first, next shortest next. Take one, Maffitt."

Maffitt didn't notice the mutterings and catcalls as Katherin in pants, brought the black up behind the others. He was watching Barr. Barr's flittery eyes were stabbing at all of them, his jaws working like a cow's on a cud. "All right, gents," the marshal spoke gruffly. "Grattison gets first ask, Harris next an' Maffitt last. Everyone got it?"

The three of them nodded. There was a second knot of men, Maffitt noticed, off to one side of the finish line a quarter mile down. The marshal's hard stare kept returning to Maffitt and now Harris' glance jolted into him with much the same look. Harris showed his teeth briefly.

"You any kin to the family of Maffitts that used to run Bridle Bit?"

"Never heard of it," Maffitt grunted.

"Could be you will, time this race gets run. Take a squint at that dun. Looks like a sure-enough winner to me."

He grinned at the scowl on Grattison's face. Grattison's horse, Snake Stomper, was a wall-eyed gray with a stripe down its back. But Hunter, dun with a red mane and tail and zebra marks about its knees, wasn't as heavily put up but had powerful hind quarters and plenty of reach. Afligido, beside them, looked gaunt as a grizzly after a hard winter.

Katherin's cheeks looked stiff but her head was high, her chin determined. She hadn't glanced at her father; not as though she were scared, more like she didn't see him, holding him away until her part in this was done. It was odd though, Maffitt thought, he hadn't spoke to her.

Maffitt's head was filled with the peril of Barr's being here in conjunction with Harris, and the marshal's dark looks, and knowing any moment this damned thing would boil over. Barr would know he was the man, and Harris would be watching him, and the marshal sooner or later was going to have to make his move.

Now the riders were waved back the full fifty feet of the score.

On both flanks the course was bounded with whitewashed rails that came up to Maffitt's belt buckle. Three saddled broncs were ground-hitched outside the nearer one and a Bridle Bit brand suggested the closest was Harris'; the others probably belonged to Barr and the local badge. Maffitt dragged his look away from them.

"Outside the rail an' grab hands, you fellers."

They got off the strip and Harris, grinning, seized Maffitt's right while Grattison, coming up on his other side, caught hold of the left. By the squeeze he put on it Maffitt wondered if Harris was trying to cripple his gun hand. The marshal tramped up to the score. Barr crossed the track and stood over there watching.

Grattison tightened his grip. Bug Hunter was showing signs of nervousness, fighting the hold on him. Afligido, sidling, had his head to the front, black barrel twisted. Only Snake Stomper was set, bunched for breaking. Grattison yelled: "Ready?"

"No!" Harris snarled. "You know better'n that! You don't ask till they're on top the startin' line!"

The marshal, tight-lipped, gave the sign and all three made a rush for the mark. Grattison yelled his question again and once more it was Harris that turned them back. The Bridle Bit boss was an old hand at this stuff. Bug Hunter, as they wheeled to return, let fly a hind hoof at the black. It missed but only the scantiest of margins. The marshal growled, "Watch it!"

Bug Hunter's jockey took a wrap in the reins but Maffitt saw his teeth flash at Katherin. A cold rage worked all through him.

Next time they came up the Breeding horse had his nose out in front and it was Harris that wanted to turn them loose and Grattison whose protest brought them around.

This, Maffitt knew, could go on for hours, but Katherin seemed to have herself well in hand. She sat relaxed in the saddle, but half

255

an hour later she was beginning to look flushed and lather made a creamy froth between her mount's cheeks and he was shaking his head. It was hard on these horses to dash into full stride and be repeatedly hauled up. The Snake tried to take a bit out of the dun and the dun, lashing out, thumped him hard in the chest. Up in the grandstand folks were beginning to get restless.

Grattison swore. "Can't that boy of yours control him?"

"Briggs," Harris said, "keep that horse in hand."

The marshal, eyes inscrutable, again waved them off. It was Grattison's ask but the Snake wasn't ready. When they came up once more Grattison's horse was in front. Afligido, lapped on Bug Hunter, was half a length to the rear and the Breeding jock was bringing the Bug around when Harris let fly with the question.

"Yes!" Grattison snarled; and Maffitt, perhaps with too much of his mind on other things, echoed Grattison's decision. The Snake lunged ahead, the crowd breaking into a wild clamor of shouting. Breeding's hard-faced jock, seemingly caught off stride, took the squealing dun in swapped lead across the black's nose, forcing Katherin to pull up.

Afligido, answering her frantic haul on the reins, plowed up the ground as he slid into a squat broadside to the course.

Suspicion told Maffitt this whole thing was no accident. The Bug was away, Breeding's jock crouched over the horse's withers; Afligido, spinning into a run, crossing the score five lengths behind.

The black was fighting for his head, Katherin almost unseated by his lightning shifts, her red hair whipping out as she struggled off-balance to get back into the saddle. Oberhorn, apoplectic, was waving his arms, yelling insanely as he ran up to Barr on the outside rail.

And it's Snake Stomper by three — came the megaphoned call, *Bug Hunter by six at the hundred and fifty!*

Maffitt put everything out of his mind but the race.

Katherin was back in the leather. "Get up on his neck!" Maffitt yelled, forgetting his words in all that din couldn't reach her. He vaulted the rail and went into a saddle, bolting the startled bronc into full gallop. Down the rail he tore behind the massed people, never seeing the marshal and the grinning Harris take after him.

Bug Hunter was coming up on the Snake with every stride. *Going into the three hundred it's Snake Stomper by a head, Bug Hunter by four, and Afligido!*

Maffitt through the wind and yelling couldn't hear but anyone could see the Snake was fully extended and running on borrowed time. Katherin was riding now, helping the black, synchronized with him, and he was into his lick, going like hell emigrating on cartwheels.

Bug Hunter, going into the four hundred, was ahead, Grattison's gray Snake commencing to wabble, mouth wide as he strained to get breath past the clog in his throat. His rider looked back as Katherin, white cheeked, took Afligido wide to go around him. Grattison's rider stood straight up in his stirrups, hauling the gray hard around into the path. The crowd came onto its feet in an uproar as the black in a blinding burst of speed skinned past by no more than the width of a stirrup. But now, plunging into soft ground by the rail, he was staggering badly.

Katherin, reins like twin straps of iron, got him back onto the strip. Ears flat he seemed almost to be flying as he went into the last forty yards scarcely a length behind the hard-pounding Bug Hunter.

The face of the Bug's jockey twisted over his shoulder. He went to the bat, arm rising and falling in a frenzy of movement that slightly threw his horse off and certainly never helped him. Afligido's black nose with its blotches of bleach pushed along the Bug's flank, came even with his shoulder. Breeding's jock, reaching out, struck Afligido between the eyes with his bat. The black momentarily faltered, running blind. Starting to drift he came suddenly out of it, eyes rolling wickedly. His ears went back, his shape stretched lower and lengthened. His pounding hoofs were like thunder as he made his final bid.

Breeding's jock tried now to crowd the Bug into them, attempting to throw the lighter horse off stride or scare the girl into pulling him off, but Afligido got his head out in front and kept it there, Breeding's jock and the girl furiously hammering each other with their bats as the horses flashed across the line.

And it's Afligido by a head!

The crowd went wild, its roar sweeping over the track like crazy. Men leaped out of the stands, shouting, cursing as they joined the rush of others scrambling like infuriated cattle toward the black knot of gesticulating officials beyond the rail behind the finish line.

Maffitt came pounding up, flinging himself from the winded pony with the marshal and Harris spurring frantically after him. The head judge was shouting blasphemously, face purple. He was a cowman who'd bet heavily and not very fortunately on Breeding's horse, but he was no shorthorn. "The black won — it don't make no difference what his damn name is! I want both them jocks! By God, I —"

Katherin came back on the heaving Afligido. There was a bright splash of crimson across the front of her neck. The crowd split to let them through and the judge took in the look of her, swearing. "Get that feller — an' Grattison's jock, too!" he rasped at a pair of burly ranch hands. "I'm goin' to get to the bottom of this! I don't care how you do it."

A gun went off somewhere. The crowd broke and scattered as more gunshots racketed through the confusion. Katherin, from her perch on Afligido, saw Maffitt trapped two rods off in the open with Harris, a smoking pistol in hand, jumping off a horse that had just pounded up.

In the sudden quiet Maffitt stood like a rock. Flame streaked again from the glint of Harris' pistol. No one saw Maffitt move but all of them heard the sound of his gun as Harris, sagging in the middle, staggered backward and went down. Somebody yelled as a horse left a chute in full career.

Maffitt, whirling, caught a glimpse of Breeding spurring hard for the open, quirting at every jump. Maffitt lunged toward the bronc he'd got off of, had very nearly reached it when the marshal with a leveled sixshooter stepped squarely in front of him.

The man's eyes were like agate.

Maffitt, sighing, stopped, letting the pistol fall to his side. "All right," he said.

It was the end of the line.

19

"Your name Maffitt?" A hand clutched his arm. "That shot hombre wants —"

"Freeze right there!" The gaping bore of the marshal's Peacemaker brooked no argument.

Somebody growled: "That was self-defense, Marshal!"

The badge toter's eyes never left Maffitt's face. There was no give to the man; with him a thing was white or black and he had already made up his mind about Maffitt. "Let go of that hoglet. Now strike out for my office."

Si Turner pushed up, Oberhorn and several hardbreathing others right on his heels. "Just a minute," Turner said. "That feller Harris was —"

"Yeah. Just like Hunsinger! I seen every bit of it," the marshal said. "I warned this slick-ear." He growled at Maffitt, "Get moving."

Over the heads of those around him Maffitt could see Katherin, still on Afligido, talking to her father. The marshal looked ominous. "Don't aim to tell you again." Maffitt, turning, was about to move off when one of the fellows bending over Harris said sharply: "Marshal! this jigger wants t' talk t' that hombre."

The marshal, frowning, finally let his breath out. "All right. Over there, Maffitt."

Harris' face when they came up was the color of damp wood ash. "That you, Maffitt? Can't see good enough to —"

"It's me," Maffitt said.

The dying man's voice, turning thin, became querulous. "Where-at's that law hound?"

"Right here holdin' a gun on me, Harris."

"Damn fool!" Harris said. "Listen — what I done was at Breedin's orders. That business . . . about your ol' man —"

He broke off, some kind of spasm shaking him. Blood came onto his lips and he went limp. Those holding him up, thinking he had had it, were easing him down when his mouth moved again. They looked at Maffitt peculiarly. "You hear that?"

Maffitt shook his head.

"Said Breeding had your dad locked up in a room, feedin' him nothin' but rotgut till the stuff finally killed him. Said this whole deal was rigged —"

"Breeding," the marshal said, "ain't here to defend himself."

"By God," Turner cried, "he *was* here! 'Bout half killed a horse gettin' —"

"I'm concerned right now with Maffitt," the marshal said, "and what *he* done *here*. What happened back there where they come from —"

"You'll never hold him for that shootin'," Oberhorn declared. "Too many of these boys seen the straight of that! If a man can't defend his own life in this town —"

"Git out of my way!" The marshal's eyes ripped a path through the crowd; his gun prodded Maffitt into it. "All this bastard's ever been is trouble. I warned him what would happen."

"Hold up a second, marshal." This was the cowman who had been presiding judge during the race. "Fetch them two right up here, boys — that's right, both of them."

The crowd began to look interested when the foremost captive was seen to be the Bug's jockey; the other man was Breeding, looking considerably the worse for wear, still trying to throw his weight around in between loud protestations of his innocence. He looked mad and scared and pretty hard used as he was hauled up in front of the scowling lawman.

"Who's this?" the badge said, and Turner grinned. Oberhorn said, "That's Breeding — a crook if I ever seen one! Now mebbe we'll git t' the bottom of this business! Ask him what deal he had fixed up with Grattison in case this black of ours —"

Growls from those around them drowned the rest of his words but the temper of these people wasn't lost on the marshal. A lot of them had damn near been ruined and all had seen what went on in that race; if Breeding had been mixed up in it the marshal couldn't afford to simply ignore the man. His cold eyes fastened on the Bug's jockey. "Talk up, you!"

Breeding's jock — the one who'd been ruled off the tracks at Chicago — licked cut lips with the whites of his eyes frittering around and hard swallowing. "I on'y done what I was told," he whined.

"Good thing for an epitaph," the judge said dryly, a thin smile quirking one side of his mouth at the sudden sick look wavering over the jock's face. "You got about one slim chance of crawlin' out of this business, and I'm tellin' you right now if you don't want to be turned over to this crowd you better talk right up an' make damn sure your tongue's straight."

The man looked pretty uncomfortable. He didn't waste any time telling everything he knew, recounting how Breeding had fetched him here to make a good thing off these suckers. He told how much Breeding had promised him if Bug Hunter got the nod for this run. He explained how Breeding had arranged, through Harris, to double every nickel Grattison had in the race if the Bug came in first. "He'd already had a race matched with this local joe — had the chump over a barrel account of the forfeit Grattison had to put up to get him here. This beef merchant seen his nag didn't have the thousandth piece of a chance when he found out the Bug was just as sound as he'd ever been. You see we'd put out this come-on about the Bug bein' lamed . . ."

The growls of those round him cut into it there and several heavy losers started for Breeding without even bothering to roll up their sleeves. Breeding, fish-belly white, let out a horrified squawk and commenced bleating his innocence and the marshal, stepping back, shifted the focus of his gun snout, the belligerents stiffening into their tracks looking balked and mean and not minded to forget it. The marshal's mouth tightened up; standing up for this skunk,

Breeding, wasn't going to endear him to anyone and, belatedly seeing this, he tried to drag Maffitt back into the limelight.

The jock, who had his own hide to think about, quickly sensing the temper of this crowd, said, "Hell, that guy's all that stood between this town and a sell-out! That black's Afligido — the pure-quill genuine article! Lot o' you figured that horse was a fake, but not Breeding; he sent Harris around to lay the law down to Maffitt. You see, back there a piece after Breeding had got rid of Maffitt's ol' man an' took the ranch over, Maffitt showed up over at Bridle Bit an' Breeding, to get him out from underfoot an' make sure he didn't turn up nothin', made him this deal to go after the black which was owned at that time by some Mexican general. Told Maffitt, Breeding did, he'd pay three thousand bucks for the horse, delivered at Bridle Bit —"

"Lies! Every bit of it lies!" Breeding shouted.

"Then you got nothing to worry about," the judge grimly said. "Go on, Briggs. Let's hear the rest of it."

"Well," the jock grinned, "Maffitt was always gettin' into some kind of scrape — had a real talent for it — and Breeding figured this wouldn't be no diff'rent. He give

Maffitt a thousand for expenses an' sent him off, thinkin' he was shed of him. So when he shows up here with the horse, Breeding had Harris tell Maffitt if the Bug didn't win they'd produce Maffitt's signature for receipt of that money an' have him jugged."

"And how do you know all this?"

"You don't think I been stickin' my neck out blind, do you? Breeding's got that receipt in his wallet this minute. He went to that cop there" — pointing at the marshal — "before the race an' got it all fixed to have this badge pick Maffitt up. Hell! you seen him an' Harris goin' after him, didn't you? Chased him the whole length of that rail! But Harris couldn't wait — he didn't want Maffitt talkin' — that's why he tried to cut him down! This guy Maffitt's square; his wife went into that race to win an' done her damndest from the start to finish. You must of seen that —"

Breeding made his bid right then. Twisting free of the pair of ranch hands holding him he tripped one of them, sending him reeling into the other, and dived into the crowd, both fists swinging. It was short and fierce before the crowd swarmed over him, literally taking him apart in their fury. Maffitt felt like retching when he heard the man's screams.

But the marshal wasn't done with this. He had his own axe to grind and a one-track mind. Through the fading din he yelled: "Barr! Come over here!"

The Bisbee sheriff didn't show much enthusiasm. Putting the best face he could on it he came reluctantly into the inner circle. "It was you," the marshal growled, "put out that dodger I got! There's your man! Take him!"

Barr licked dry lips. "No charges," he said and Katherin, coming up with Afligido in tow, grinned through the dust and caught Maffitt's hand.

The marshal ripped off his badge and flung it down in disgust. "You don't need no law," he snarled at those nearest — "what you need is a keeper!"

Katherin, still hanging onto Maffitt, hugged his arm against her. "How far is Bridle Bit?" and, when he told her, "Hadn't we better get started?"

She was a powerful lot of woman, one to keep a man stirred up, Maffitt reckoned, but after all they had lately been through he guessed together they could handle whatever else life had to offer. "There's just one thing," he said. "From here on out I'll be wearin' the pants."

We hope you have enjoyed this Large Print book. Other Thorndike Press or Chivers Press Large Print books are available at your library or directly from the publishers.

For more information about current and upcoming titles, please call or write, without obligation, to:

Thorndike Press
295 Kennedy Memorial Drive
Waterville, ME 04901

(800) 223-1244
(800) 223-6121

OR

Chivers Press Limited
Windsor Bridge Road
Bath BA2 3AX
England
Tel. (0225) 335336

All our Large Print titles are designed for easy reading, and all our books are made to last.